Naomi stared ~~at the~~ **st strip, hardly** ~~believing what~~ **he was seeing**

She blinked several times, but this wasn't a dream. No matter how long she gazed at the test strip, the red plus sign remained clear as day.

Stunned, she tried to wrap her mind around the news. How could this have happened? Their protection had only failed once. The timing hadn't been right. And even if the timing had been right, her doctor had explained about the scar tissue and how it would impact her ability to get pregnant.

With all the strikes against her, how could she have gotten pregnant at the wrong time?

She swallowed hard, putting a hand to her stomach. The overwhelming exhaustion. The never-ending nausea. The constant going to the bathroom.

Everything made sense now.

This baby was a miracle. Despite her upset stomach, she grinned like a fool. A true miracle. The thrill of excitement faded.

Rick. How on earth was she going to tell him?

Her knees gave out and she sat down, feeling dizzy. After the way they'd parted in Chicago, she didn't think he'd take the news well. He wasn't ready to think about the future. He wasn't ready for a family.

Dear Reader,

Giving birth to a baby is a magical, awe-inspiring experience. But what if you'd dedicated your life, your career, to saving others instead of listening to your biological clock? Such is the case of trauma surgeon Naomi Horton.

Naomi has always planned on having a family, but a painful miscarriage and subsequent divorce has left her devastated. She's even considered artificial insemination, since the only man she's even remotely attracted to happens to be her new boss, Dr. Rick Weber, chief of Trauma surgery. Naomi wants a baby, not a man, and Rick is definitely off limits.

Rick has also suffered a tragic loss, and having a family isn't a part of his future plans—until a secret affair with Naomi results in a surprise pregnancy. Can these two wounded souls heal each other and create a new family of their own?

I hope you enjoy *The Surgeon's Secret Baby Wish*. I always enjoy hearing from my readers, so please visit my Web site and drop me a note.

Happy Reading!

Laura Iding

www.lauraiding.com

THE SURGEON'S SECRET BABY WISH
Laura Iding

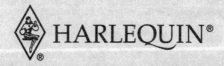

TORONTO • NEW YORK • LONDON
AMSTERDAM • PARIS • SYDNEY • HAMBURG
STOCKHOLM • ATHENS • TOKYO • MILAN • MADRID
PRAGUE • WARSAW • BUDAPEST • AUCKLAND

ISBN-13: 978-0-373-19921-1
ISBN-10:   0-373-19921-X

THE SURGEON'S SECRET BABY WISH

First North American Publication 2008

THE SURGEON'S SECRET BABY WISH

This book is dedicated to my sister-in-law
Sarah Iding, because she loves babies.

CHAPTER ONE

HE WOULD be the perfect man to father her baby.

Dr Rick Weber was tall, had brilliant blue eyes, thick chestnut-colored hair and a lean, muscular build. Just looking at him made her mouth go dry. His gaze collided with hers and the air crackled with tension for countless seconds when their eyes locked. He was the first to look away and it took a moment for her to resume breathing.

Shaken, she stared at him. He would have been perfect. Except for one tiny problem.

Rick Weber happened to be the new chief of pediatric trauma surgery.

And her new boss.

Dr Naomi Horton pulled herself together, hoping her moment of insane unprofessionalism wasn't evident on her features. What was wrong with her?

She straightened in her seat, all too aware that she was one of only two female pediatric trauma surgeons in the conference room, and Debra Maloney didn't count as she was happily married. Naomi didn't think it was likely that any of the other four trauma surgeons would be drooling over their new boss.

"Good morning. Thanks for coming in on such short notice." Rick appeared calm and relaxed as he addressed the group. If he was intimidated by his new position, leading a group of peds trauma surgeons, some of whom had been at the job much longer than he had, he didn't show it. She took a bracing sip of her coffee, anxious for the kick of caffeine. She hadn't slept well the night before, irrationally nervous about their first early morning meeting as she hadn't yet met their new boss.

"I know we have our level one trauma center review coming up next week," Rick continued. He swept a glance over the group. "Are there any outstanding issues I need to be aware of?"

Naomi couldn't think of anything major, but she was the most junior member of the trauma team, having only been on staff at Children's Memorial Hospital for two years. She remained silent as two of the tenured surgeons, Frank Turner and Chuck Lowrey, mentioned a few problem areas and the steps they'd taken to mitigate them.

She listened to the discussion but her mind began to drift, her gaze unerringly coming back to rest on Rick.

Why was she so physically aware of him? She hadn't so much as experienced anything more than a flicker of interest in a man since her divorce two years ago. Why now? And why her new boss? A man completely off-limits?

Was fate trying to tell her something?

No, she needed to maintain a positive attitude. Her divorce had been rough. She and Andrew, her ex-husband, had both wanted a baby for a long time. But after suffering a devastating miscarriage, and then being told that her ability to conceive again was unlikely, their relationship had quickly fallen apart.

One night she'd come home from work to find Andrew had packed up and moved out. She'd tried to talk to him, to salvage their marriage, but Andrew hadn't been interested.

Her divorce hadn't eliminated her desire to have a child, though. She'd gotten pregnant once before so she knew it could happen again. And she just couldn't believe she was destined to live her life without ever having a baby. A child to love and cherish. Even if it meant raising a child on her own.

Rick described his plans to upgrade their trauma program, including monthly quality reviews on surgical complications, and she took notes, hoping the task would break the visceral reaction he seemed to have on her.

His gaze brushed hers and her pulse kicked into triple digits. She glanced away, hoping she could get her hormones to settle down soon.

This was ridiculous. Yes, she fantasized about having a baby, but having a real-life, flesh-and-blood man wasn't a part of her plan. Her marriage had crumbled at the time she'd needed Andrew the most. She refused to open herself up to that sort of pain again.

Which left only one option. Artificial insemination.

She'd debated long and hard, finally choosing a donor, paying her money and scheduling an appointment at the fertilization clinic. That had been four months ago. Minor crises at work had kept making her miss the appointments and her cycle was irregular, which didn't help either.

She was ovulating again, so she'd made another appointment. This time she refused to let anything get in her way.

"Any questions?" Rick's gaze locked with hers. A guilty flush stained her cheeks. Could he tell she hadn't been paying attention? Or, worse, could he tell how much his mere presence affected her?

She gathered her scattered, sleep-deprived thoughts. What had he talked about? She glanced at her notes. Oh, yes, plans for expanding their pediatric trauma prevention program into the community. She cleared her throat. "Do you need a volunteer to be on the community education committee? Because, if so, I'd like to be involved."

"Absolutely." Rick's face lit up. "Naomi Horton, right?"

She nodded, feeling her heart race at the sound of her name in his deep, husky voice. Good grief, she hadn't worked so hard to get through five years of surgical residency followed by another year as a surgical/trauma fellow to react like an adolescent the first time a gorgeous man smiled at her. She'd worked darned hard to get where she was and she wasn't about to do anything to jeopardize her position.

"I've met the rest of the team over these past few days, but kept missing you. Glad to finally put a face to a name." Rick's tone turned serious. "Yes, the community education program is very important to our trauma recertification process. I appreciate your willingness to help out."

"No problem."

"Great." His gaze lingered on hers for a moment and she had the impression there was a hint of sadness in them before he turned and glanced over the group. "Any other questions?" He paused, waiting. "If not, we'll call this meeting adjourned. Uh, Naomi, do you have a minute?"

Feeling like the errant student who hadn't finished her homework, Naomi stood awkwardly to the side, allowing her colleagues to pass by on their way out of the physician conference room.

"What's up?" she asked, striving for a distant tone. "I'm on service today in the PICU and need to get upstairs to make rounds."

"I know, but I need a favor." For the first time that morning, Rick appeared ill at ease.

A favor? She lifted a curious brow. "What?"

"I need someone to cover my call shift this evening." His gaze was slightly apologetic. "I have a pressing personal issue I need to take care of. I can take over about nine o'clock or ten at the latest, if that's all right with you?"

Nine or ten? Her heart sank. Heck no, it wasn't all right. She had an appointment at the clinic at six and they closed at eight. Was he asking her because she was the most junior member of the group? Or because she was divorced and couldn't possibly have a life? She stiffened her spine, not willing to be viewed as the easy mark. No way was she going to start covering all Rick's call shifts, just because he happened to be the boss. She swallowed hard and forced a tight smile. "I'm sorry, but I have plans this evening. You'll have to ask someone else."

"I see." He simply looked at her for a moment, but then slowly nodded. "I understand. I did check with the others. Debra is already post-call and she was up most of the night. Steve and Dirk are flying out to San Francisco to attend a national pediatric trauma conference. Frank and his wife are celebrating their twentieth wedding anniversary, and Chuck Lowrey is filling in for one of the general surgeons while he's on vacation."

Damn. That pretty much covered their entire team. But her plans were just as important as anyone else's. More so, because every time she canceled it meant another month of waiting. Another month of postponing her dream of having a family of her own. Helplessly she lifted a shoulder. "I'm sorry."

His smile was crooked. "It's all right. My problem, not yours. Thanks anyway."

She turned away, fully intending to walk out, but the way he'd accepted her decision, without pulling rank or asking specifically what her plans were, made her waver. What was his pressing personal issue? She'd heard through the grapevine that Rick wasn't married, but that didn't mean anything. No doubt he was in some sort of relationship. For all she knew, his plans might not be anything more than getting his girlfriend settled after their move.

Yet to be fair, he didn't seem like the type to exaggerate his need for time off. Trauma surgeons knew being on call was a part of the job, and being in charge of the program meant you had to take call rotations like everyone else. She took one step toward the door, and then another. She stopped. Calling herself every kind of fool, she sighed and turned back to meet Rick's faintly questioning gaze. "I'll take your shift."

For a moment his eyes lit up but then he shook his head. "No, I can't ask you to cancel your plans."

"It's not a big deal." Sure. No big deal, just her entire future. She stifled a sigh and forced a smile. "Really, take care of what you need to do. I'll cover your call."

There was a long pause, as if he were debating with himself on whether or not he should take her up on her offer. Finally he nodded. "Thanks, Naomi. And if you get slammed with patients, just give me a call and I'll back you up. With any luck, I'll be finished by nine."

Usually Wednesday nights weren't exactly big trauma nights, unless the weather was bad. Peds trauma wasn't nearly as busy as adult trauma. She was supposed to be second call anyway, but had figured there'd be little chance of being called in to help Rick, so she'd made the appointment when she'd realized she was ovulating.

If she didn't go to the clinic today, she wouldn't be able to go for the rest of the week. She and the other surgeons had picked up extra shifts to cover for Steve and Dirk who were on their way to San Francisco.

Canceling her plans tonight meant she'd forgo her chance of getting pregnant this month. Just like she'd forgone her plans last month and the month before that.

Her heart squeezed in her chest. She needed to find

a way to make regular appointments and keep them. Her OB doctor had warned her that conceiving would be difficult, thanks to the scar tissue she'd sustained during several bouts of endometriosis. Canceling her appointments wasn't helping in her quest to get pregnant.

"Thanks again," Rick said, his gaze warm with appreciation. "I owe you one."

"Sure." Her smile was weak. He might owe her a favor but there was no way she could ask him to provide the one thing she really wanted.

A baby.

Rick watched Naomi leave, then yanked his gaze away when he realized he was admiring her petite, yet curvy backside. He frowned and gave his head a slight shake. He wasn't interested in women, not any more.

Not ever again.

Convincing himself he'd only been grateful because Naomi had bailed him out of a jam, he stood. Rubbing a hand over the back of his neck, he headed back to his office to catch up on his e-mails until the hour was late enough that he could call his sister.

Forty-five minutes later, he picked up the phone. "Jess? I managed to get off work tonight, so I can go to the father-daughter dance with Lizzy."

"Oh, Rick, that's wonderful. Lizzy will be ecstatic." Jessica hesitated, then added, "Are you sure you're going to be okay? I know this won't be easy for you."

"I'm fine." He knew he sounded gruff, but couldn't help it. Two years and the pain of his loss hadn't gone away. Although sometimes he could go for days without thinking about it. He cleared his throat and tried to soften his tone. "Lizzy deserves to have someone escort her to the father-daughter dance. I'm honored to take her."

"She's going to be so thrilled. Thanks for rearranging your schedule, Rick."

"No problem. Tell Lizzy I'll pick her up at six." He hung up the phone and stared blindly at his computer. He wasn't so sure Naomi would appreciate why he'd asked her to cover his shift, but he couldn't regret taking up her offer. Lizzy had just turned ten and was feeling left out of the "in" crowd at school. But she was a great kid, and it certainly wasn't her fault she hadn't seen her father for years. The jerk had taken off shortly after Lizzy's birth.

Jess had done a good job of raising Lizzy alone, but he also knew his sister had struggled. He'd helped Jess financially, but it hadn't been until recently, after he'd lost his own wife and child, that he'd begun looking for a position to bring him closer to home.

A new start was just what he needed to help get away from the memories. Plus, he figured he should help Jess raise Lizzy, as they didn't have any other family left. And he wasn't interested in going down that path again. Having and losing one family in a lifetime was bad enough.

Rick left work early so he could catch a couple of hours' sleep, just in case he had a busy call night. He didn't sleep well, but managed to get a little rest. He showered and dressed, then left to pick up his niece.

The father-daughter dance wasn't nearly as bad as he'd expected. The gym of the elementary school had been decorated with streams of crepe paper and dozens of balloons. The disc jockey played songs, took requests and held a dance contest. He and Lizzy participated but his lack of coordination hindered their chance of winning. He managed to participate in the chicken dance, though, and if he felt like an idiot, flapping his arms like wings, he considered it lucky that no one he knew was around to see him.

For a few songs the DJ played some sort of rap music that hurt his ears. Thankfully, the girls preferred dancing with each other, leaving the dads and surrogate dads to stand around, awkwardly talking about sports and wishing for something stronger than punch to drink. He caught himself glancing at his watch and wondering how Naomi was doing. For her sake, he hoped the trauma calls weren't too bad.

Finally, the DJ announced the last song, and he danced once again with Lizzy. Her head barely reached his chest, but they managed to get through the whole number without him stepping on her toes.

"Thanks, Uncle Rick," she murmured, gazing up at him with wide, adoring brown eyes. "I'm so glad you could come with me. I was so sad to think I might have to sit at home alone tonight."

The thought of Lizzy feeling sad and lonely made him doubly glad Naomi had helped him out. "Hey, I'm the lucky guy who got to dance with the most beautiful girl in the world."

"Oh, brother." She rolled her eyes, but blushed and giggled. "You always say that."

"Because it's true." He took her hand as they headed

toward the door, and glanced down at her. "I love you, Lizzy."

"I love you too, Uncle Rick." She flashed him a dazzling smile, and just for a moment he imagined that his daughter Sarah would have looked at him in the same way, six years from now.

A sharp stab of pain caught him off guard and he dropped his car keys. Fumbling, he picked them up and then held the door for Lizzy so they could walk outside. A thick fog hung over the school parking lot, so he used the key fob to help locate their car.

Pulling himself out from under a cloak of painful memories, he helped Lizzy inside and then walked around to the driver's side. He started the car and carefully drove out of the parking lot, moving slowly because of the dense fog. Luckily his sister's house wasn't far. He was headed in that direction when his pager went off.

With a frown, he pulled the car over and read the text message from Naomi. *Multi-vehicle crash with five peds victims expected, one DOA at the scene. I'm going to need help.*

"Is there a problem?" Lizzy asked, her freckle-dusted nose wrinkling in a frown.

"Yeah, I'm going to have to go back to the hospital tonight." Still driving slowly, keeping a careful eye out for other cars, he pulled into his sister's driveway and left the car running while he took the time to see Lizzy safely inside the house. "See you later, kiddo." He gave her a quick hug. "Tell your mom I'll call her tomorrow."

"I will. Bye. Thanks again." Lizzy waved as he dashed to his car and backed out of the driveway.

Adrenaline surged as he drove toward Children's Memorial, the short ride taking twice as long as usual. He didn't doubt that the heavy fog had contributed to the MVA. Five peds victims was almost unheard of when the average was a couple calls a night. He supposed he should be thankful that the crash had taken place after Lizzy's father-daughter dance had ended.

Fifteen minutes later he strode into the E.D. and found Naomi up to her pretty neck in pediatric trauma victims. There were three youngsters in the trauma room, ages ranging from eight to fourteen, each looking worse than the next.

A wave of guilt for asking Naomi to switch shifts with him hit him.

"Where do you want me to start?" he asked. Naomi was still the surgeon in charge, and he didn't want to automatically take control of the situation she'd already begun to handle.

"Take a look at the youngest over there." She pointed to the victims closest to the door. "I think he needs to go to the O.R. We're going to have to split up, one operating on patients while the other continues triaging patients down here."

He glanced around, noting the level of activity. "Split up? Are you sure that's a good idea?"

"We don't have a choice." Naomi's gaze was grim. "These are only the first three victims—there are still two more on the way. We need to clear a few of these patients out of here before the next ones arrive."

CHAPTER TWO

NAOMI wished she could have avoided bothering Rick, but there were too many victims for one trauma surgeon to handle. This many pediatric trauma patients was unusual, but apparently there was a special kids' night being held at the baseball park and lots of kids had been in the cars that had crashed. As she was already triaging, she decided to send Rick to surgery.

"You'd better take this patient to the O.R." She gestured to the youngest patient, Jimmy Dupont, an eight-year-old with a tense abdomen. "I'm pretty sure he has a ruptured spleen, he's lost too much blood. If you can take him off my hands, I'll manage the rest of the triage down here."

"All right." Rick didn't argue, but motioned to the nurse hanging another unit of blood. "Let's go. I'll change clothes when we get to the O.R."

In the back corner of her mind she realized Rick was wearing a suit and tie, but there wasn't time to resent how he'd used her to cover for a hot date, not when she had so many patients to care for. She turned her attention to the situation at hand, feeling as if she was standing in the middle of a war zone.

"All right, I want the twelve-year-old female, Chelsey Dupont, transferred to the ICU." She'd already intubated Chelsey and placed a chest tube for the girl's collapsed lung. Out of all the trauma patients they'd received so far, Chelsey had been the first to arrive and was the most stable of the bunch. The PICU residents upstairs could handle her care for a little while.

"I want Tristan Brown to get a CT scan of his chest and belly." She suspected fourteen-year-old Tristan had a severe liver laceration, but needed to make sure it was nothing more. He also had a compound femur fracture and had already called the ortho surgeons to take a look at him.

"Doc?" Tristan reached out for her as the nurses began to wheel him away.

"What is it, Tristan?" She stopped them, and took his hand. "What's wrong?"

"Where's my sister? Where's Emily?"

She bit her lip, hoping to heaven that Emily wasn't the child who'd been declared DOA on the scene. "I don't know. How old is she? There are still a few victims on the way."

"Seven. Emily is only seven." Tristan's eyes were wild with anxiety. "You have to find her for me. Our parents were hurt, too. I need to see Emily."

The whole family. She swallowed hard and gently squeezed his hand. "I'll find Emily but we need to take care of you, too, Tristan. The nurses are going to take you to Radiology for a CT scan of your belly. I need to make sure there's nothing more serious than a few broken bones."

"I don't care." His eyes filled with anguished tears.

"Find Emily, Doc. Please, find my sister. Tell her I love her."

"I will." She released his hand and stepped back so the nurses could wheel him away. She bit her lip, desperately needing to find out the name of the DOA patient. She didn't know if the DOA was an adult or a child, and although no one deserved to die in a car crash, she found herself praying the dead patient wasn't little Emily.

She hurried towards the unit clerk's desk but was brought up short when the doors to the trauma room burst open and two more bloodstained patients were brought in.

Fleeting panic hit low in her belly. Never in her life had she ever faced such a massive influx of pediatric trauma patients at one time. She strove to remain calm, listening as the paramedics rattled off the pertinent details.

"Ten-year-old male with multiple fractures, including his pelvis, long extrication at the scene, blood pressure low-eighties over forty."

"Do you have a name?" She wanted to know how many families they were dealing with here. So far they had the Duponts and the Browns.

"Mike Winthrop."

Make that a third family. She filed that bit of information away for when the family members started coming in. "Start fluid resuscitation until Ortho gets here." Naomi glanced at the second patient. With all the blood covering the child's face, it was difficult to determine the gender. "What's the story with this one?"

"Crushing chest injury, and another long extrication

at the scene. The car that hit them was on top of their car, crushing the victims in the back seat."

"Age and name?"

"Emily Brown. We almost had to sedate her brother who wasn't doing very well himself yet was still trying to crawl back into the car to get her."

Having just spoken to Tristan, she wasn't surprised. Her gaze landed on Emily and she swallowed her fear, knowing the massive injuries stretched her limitations as a trauma surgeon. "Call the cardiothoracic surgeons, I need someone here to evaluate her asap."

One of the nurses scurried off. Naomi did a quick examination of Emily, but she could see the poor girl's ribs flailing from the foot of the gurney. Dear God most if not all of her ribs were broken. She hated to think of the damage that had already been done to her small heart. Most of the trauma surgeons could do a little open-chest surgery, but she'd only done it a couple of times and never alone. Given a choice, she'd rather have the experts with her.

"The CT surgeon is on his way in from home, but the weather may cause him to be delayed," the nurse informed her a few minutes later. "He said he'd get here as soon as possible."

She blew out a breath. No choice. Emily was her patient. "Okay, we can't waste any more time. Get those labs sent off and we'll take her straight up to surgery."

"What about Mike Winthrop?" Missy, the charge nurse, asked, a harried expression on her face.

"Get the ortho trauma team to write the admitting orders on both Tristan Brown with his multiple fractures and Mike Winthrop with his crushed pelvis. Get them ICU beds and either Rick or I will be up to see them as soon as we're finished in the O.R."

"Okay." Missy bustled off. Naomi didn't waste any more time, but headed up to the O.R. with little Emily.

The O.R. team had Emily prepped, draped and ready to go. Anesthesia was there, putting the seven-year-old to sleep and monitoring her labile vital signs. Naomi scrubbed at the sinks outside the room and then donned her sterile garb. Her stomach clenched and she was glad she hadn't eaten much for dinner because she felt sick at the thought of doing this alone. Taking a deep breath, she entered the O.R. suite.

"Ready?" she asked, taking her place at the patient's chest. She wasn't tall, and she generally used a step stool to perform surgery, which everyone had pretty much gotten used to by now.

"We've been giving blood as fast as possible, but she's not gaining any ground," the anesthesiologist warned. His name was Matt Granger and she'd done many cases with him before.

"Keep doing what you're doing, and let's see what we have." Naomi reached for a scalpel and made the incision straight down the center of Emily's small chest.

Her ribs were a mess and she didn't need to cut the sternum as it was already broken. "Suction," she barked when blood gushed, obliterating her view of the heart. Sweat trickled down the center of her back. "I need to find the source of her bleeding."

"Need a hand?" a deep voice asked from behind her. She turned to see Rick standing there.

She wanted nothing more than to have Rick's help,

but the other five trauma patients needed him, too. And it was possible that Emily's heart was beyond repair. No sense in putting the other patients at risk by tying up both of them. "I'm fine for now. The CT surgeon is on his way in from home. You'd better go and check out the ICU admissions. All of the trauma patients have been admitted to the ICU, the ortho trauma team should be evaluating the two with major fractures."

"Sounds like everything is under control." He gestured to the open chest. "Are you comfortable with this?"

"I've only done open-chest procedures a few times," she admitted, "but hopefully I'll find the bleeder." She turned back to her patient and examined the chest cavity as well as she could, thinking it was possible Emily had a tear in her inferior vena cava, one of the major veins carrying blood to the heart.

"I'll check on the ICU patients and then come back," Rick said, his voice fading as he moved away. She didn't bother to respond. If Emily's vena cava was torn, things were going to get worse before they got better.

More suction, and she still couldn't quite pinpoint the source of the hemorrhage.

"We're losing her. I have maximum doses of three different vasopressors running with no response in blood pressure," Matt informed her.

"Give more blood." Sweat pooled at the base of her spine as she fought to slow the bleeding. The vena cava wasn't an artery but its proximity to the heart made things tricky. "Does anyone know when the CT surgeon will arrive?" she asked, hoping the tremor in her voice didn't betray her.

"I'll check." The circulating nurse left.

There was way too much blood. If she didn't do something to get the bleeding under control soon, this poor little girl would die. "I want her placed on the heart-lung bypass machine."

Matt's gaze met hers over the supine body of their patient. "Are you sure?"

"I don't have a choice. I can't fix the tear in her vena cava without additional support for her heart."

The second circulating nurse in the room wheeled in the heart-lung bypass machine. Naomi was out of her depth with the extent of this surgery and she knew it. "Call Dr Weber back, tell him I need help."

"I spoke with Dr Yulton, the CT surgeon on call. He'll be here in ten minutes."

She wasn't sure Emily had ten minutes to spare, but she nodded to indicate she'd heard. The techs set up the bypass machine while she began to cross-clamp the major arteries in preparation for the switch-over.

"I'm here." Rick's voice had never sounded so good.

"I'm losing her," she said, her voice steady. "The CT surgeon will be here soon, but I need help now."

Rick didn't say a word but helped her perform the switch to bypass. They managed to get Emily safely transferred to the heart-lung machine just as the pediatric cardio thoracic surgeon walked in.

Naomi didn't leave, but was more than happy to let the CT surgeon take the lead. Rick stayed too, and once

Craig Yulton got Emily's bleeding under control, she breathed a little easier.

"I'll take her from here," Craig said, glancing up at Naomi from the opposite side of the patient. "I heard about the multi-car crash after the ballgame, so I'm sure you have other patients to see."

They did, so Naomi nodded gratefully and stepped down off her stool away from the table. Rick followed her out of the O.R. suite.

They stripped off their face masks simultaneously. The post-adrenaline rush hit hard and she struggled to breathe.

"Are you all right?" he asked, his voice full of concern.

She tried to nod, but her knees trembled and she suddenly felt weak. Taking a few steps, she sank into the nearest chair and buried her face in her hands.

"Naomi?" Rick's hand on her shoulder was warm, when she was cold inside and out.

"I almost lost her." Regret for every minute she'd wasted burned in the back of her throat. She took a deep breath and tried to pull herself together, but kept remembering how she'd sent Rick back to the ICU when she really should have handed Emily's care over to him. "I let my ego get in the way and I almost lost her."

"What are you talking about?" Rick asked in an incredulous tone. "You did everything exactly right. It was your decision to put her on bypass."

"Too late. I should have made the decision sooner." She lifted her head, forcing herself to meet Rick's puzzled gaze. "I should have asked you to stay. I've never done an open-chest case on my own." The truth weighed on her shoulders like a truckload of bricks and she glanced down, noticing how badly her hands were shaking yet powerless to make them stop. "It's my fault if Emily dies."

Rick stared at Naomi, realizing she was completely serious. Her hands were shaking and she was truly upset. Pediatrics wasn't an easy specialty, not when their small patients had so much life yet to live. But even so he couldn't remember the last time he'd seen a surgeon take a patient's outcome so personally. "No, it's not. Five pediatric trauma cases is a major disaster. There were several adults we sent over to Trinity, too. You did everything possible to save each and every patient. If this young girl dies, it's because a car landed on her, not because of anything you did or didn't do."

She shook her head, refusing to believe him.

His heart ached for her, and if they were handing out blame, he knew he deserved a large portion for himself. If he hadn't convinced Naomi to switch shifts with him, he would have been the one in charge and would have stayed in the trauma room to triage patients. The seven-year-old with the crushing chest wound would have ended up as his patient. But he didn't honestly think he could have handled the surgery very differently than Naomi had. Heck, it was always easy to second-guess yourself after the fact, dissecting every little thing you could have done differently.

"We'd better get over to the ICU," Naomi said in a

low voice, clearly struggling to pull herself together. "There's still a lot of work to do."

She was right. They did have a lot of work yet to do, but he couldn't stand to see her beating herself up like this. Especially when she didn't deserve it. He took her hands and drew her to her feet. Naomi was a tiny thing, her figure hidden by the baggy O.R. scrubs, but he could see silky wisps of her ebony hair escaping the edges of her cap. There was something about her that drew him to her, something he couldn't ignore. He gave her hands a gentle squeeze. "Naomi, you're an excellent surgeon."

"Thanks." She didn't meet his eyes and he knew she was simply being polite. She didn't believe he meant what he said.

He had the crazy urge to fold her into his arms for a reassuring hug, but held himself in check. After all, he was her boss and he barely knew her, only having met her for the first time at their meeting that morning. He willed her to see he was telling the truth. "I'm not handing you a line, Naomi. I haven't been here long, but this situation tonight would have put immense pressure on any member of the team. I'm impressed."

"You wouldn't be so impressed if one of the more experienced members of the team was here," she pointed out. "I just happen to be the youngest and least experienced surgeon on staff."

"No, actually, I'm most impressed because of how much you care." Rick released her hands and took a step back, knowing he was treading on dangerous ground. For too long he'd been so lost in his own misery he hadn't allowed anyone close. Hadn't allowed himself to care about anyone except his sister Jess and his niece Lizzy. Yet suddenly, here with Naomi, he was feeling dangerously vulnerable. "You're a trauma surgeon who truly cares. I think some of us tend to keep ourselves distant from our patients."

She tilted her head, regarding him warily. "I guess I can understand. I mean, you've been treating pediatric trauma patients for years and after a while I'm sure it's difficult to handle the loss."

He swallowed hard, wishing he could tell her the truth. Was surprised he even wanted to. But he couldn't force the words out of his throat. His wife and daughter were buried too deep in his soul to let them free. "Losing children is never easy." He was impressed his voice was so steady when Sarah's face was etched so clearly in his mind. "Now, come on, we have patients to see."

She didn't smile, but nodded and fell into step beside him as they headed out of the operating room and down the hall toward the pediatric ICU. She didn't say much until they entered the unit, and then she began asking questions about the newest patients.

Together they made rounds, making sure all aspects of care were covered. They saw Tristan last, and he watched as Naomi approached his bedside. "Tristan, Emily is here at the hospital, in surgery."

Tristan couldn't respond verbally—they'd been forced to intubate him during the CT scan. The kid had a pretty severe grade-four liver laceration and multiple fractures. But Rick noticed the teenager clung to Naomi's hand.

"Emily's heart had a small tear next to it, and many

of her ribs were broken, but she's doing okay. You need to rest, Tristan, so you can be strong for Emily."

The boy nodded and after a few minutes, Naomi reassuringly patted his hand and stepped back. After they'd reviewed Tristan's orders, they headed down to the nurses' station.

"Emily Brown is coming out of the O.R. in fifteen minutes," the unit clerk informed them.

"I'll stay until she's settled in," Naomi said.

Rick glanced at his watch, not surprised to see it was well after midnight. "Naomi, you can't. You really need to go home and get some sleep. You're on call tomorrow night, aren't you?"

She nodded, fatigue evident on her face. "Yeah, I'm covering for Dirk. Another half-hour isn't going to matter one way or the other. I want to see her before I go home."

Suspecting more arguments would be useless, he gave up. He would have offered to take her call shift, but had a bad feeling he was going to be up most of the night as it was.

He helped himself to a cup of coffee and then headed down to bed fourteen, where Emily was due to be placed. The CT team had brought her out quicker than the promised fifteen minutes and he stood beside Naomi, watching as they settled Emily.

The young girl was stable, her heart was doing as well as could be expected. All they could do now was to wait and see.

"Go home, Naomi," Rick said in a low tone. "I'll be here with her all night."

"I know." She flashed a small smile and he was

struck by how beautiful she truly was. His chest squeezed tight. "Promise you'll call if you need anything."

"I will." He shoved his hands deep into the pockets of his lab coat as she turned and walked away, her shoulders slumped beneath the weight of her guilt.

He stood watching her leave, wishing she didn't have to go. He liked working with her. Scary, considering he'd revealed more of himself to Naomi than he had to anyone else over the past two years, since he'd lost his wife and two-year-old daughter.

He shook his head. Since Gabrielle and Sarah had died, he'd kept his emotions in deep freeze. He'd stayed in peds because starting over in another specialty hadn't appealed to him, but he kept himself emotionally isolated from everyone. It had been the only way he'd been able to survive.

Emily's sweet face reminded him painfully of his daughter's. Innocent Sarah, far too young to die. He blocked the image the best he could as he went to work.

But somehow he couldn't find his usual, comfortable emotional distance. His feelings were already involved.

With Emily.

And especially with Naomi.

CHAPTER THREE

N<small>AOMI</small> tried to sleep in the following morning, especially since she was off work until five o'clock when it would be time for her to take over her call shift.

But she woke up every hour, starting at seven in the morning, and finally gave up at ten. She dragged herself out of bed, knowing there was no way she'd manage to get any rest until she went back to the hospital to follow up on her trauma admissions from the night before.

Especially Emily. And Tristan. Had their parents survived the crash? She hoped there was someone close to them who could come and support them during this time of crisis.

After taking a quick shower, she dried her hair, appreciating the ease of her simple, chin-length bob. She didn't use much make-up, especially when she was only going to be on call later anyway. She pulled on a pair of trim black trousers and an electric-blue blouse topped with her white lab coat. Outside, the sun was shining brightly, no sign of the heavy fog from the night before that had caused such devastation after the baseball game.

Her house wasn't far from Children's Memorial Hospital. For practical reasons she preferred to live close to the hospital. After Andrew had left, she'd kept the house as she'd paid most of the mortgage anyway. He hadn't argued, happy to take the cash buyout, which hadn't been a surprise considering how hard he'd tried to convince her they'd needed to move to a bigger and better place outside the city limits.

Reminders of her ex-husband made her frown. She'd been devastated at losing their baby, and when Andrew had moved out during one of her extended call shifts, she'd been shocked. How could he have been so cold? So callous?

When she'd tried to talk to him, he'd told her he'd been thinking of leaving her anyway, because of her erratic schedule and long hours. The discovery of her infertility had convinced him there was no hope for them. He hadn't wanted to go through the stress and agony all over again.

As much as she'd tried to tell herself she was obviously better off without him, she had never felt so lonely.

Naomi pulled into the designated private parking garage reserved for physicians and shook off thoughts of Andrew as she strode into the hospital. She didn't bother with the elevator but took the stairs to the third-floor pediatric intensive care unit.

Rick was standing at the main desk when she walked in and he glanced at the clock with a puzzled frown. "You're a little early, aren't you?"

"Couldn't sleep." She lifted a shoulder in a half-shrug, feeling self-conscious after the way she'd gotten so emotional on him last night. "How are things going?"

"So far, good." Rick's gaze slid from hers and her gut clenched, knowing he was holding something back. With unspoken agreement, they walked down the hall towards the physician conference room.

"Emily? How's Emily doing?"

Rick didn't say anything but steered her toward the conference room, which for once was empty of residents. He turned to face her, his expression grim. "She had a rough night, Naomi. They've decided to place her on the heart transplant list."

"What?" Shocked, she could only stare at him. "She needs a new heart? How? Why?"

He nodded. "They took her back to surgery this morning, because she'd continued to bleed. During the surgery they decided they didn't have any choice but to put her on a Heartmate."

A Heartmate was an external device that took over the work of the heart. It was often used as a bridge to a transplant. But pediatric organs were rarely available. It was possible that Emily would be forced to live much of her life on the device. If she could manage to avoid a life-threatening infection, that was.

"Poor Emily." She had to blink back tears. "Does her family know? Tristan?"

"Her parents are patients at Trinity Medical Center, but the nurses in the ICU over there brought Emily's mother over during the night. Emily's father was too sick to be moved."

The poor family. How awful to be hospitalized in different places. Especially when Emily's life hung in the balance. "If she dies, it's my fault."

Rick sighed and scrubbed a hand over the back of

his neck. "Naomi, don't do this to yourself. Emily was crushed by a car. If she dies, it's not your fault."

Yes, it would be her fault, but there was no point in arguing. The trauma department had a monthly morbidity and mortality review, and this case would certainly be discussed, along with her performance during surgery. The best thing a surgeon could do was to own up to their mistakes and learn from them. The fact that Emily would have died without the Heartmate was serious enough.

"Naomi?" She started, realizing Rick had been talking to her, his blue eyes bright with concern. "Are you sure you're all right?"

"I'm fine."

"You saved the lives of five pediatric trauma patients last night. Don't the others count at all?" his exasperated tone grated on her nerves. "Give yourself a break, would you? Or were you responsible for the DOA on the scene, too?"

She grit her teeth, knowing he was right, even if she didn't appreciate his sarcasm. "Yes, the other patients do count." She pulled herself together, knowing Emily was still alive. Maybe a miracle would happen and the youngster would get a new heart, sooner rather than later. "How are the families dealing with everything?"

"As well as can be expected. As you know, both Brown parents are patients in the adult ICU at Trinity, and so is the father of the Dupont family. The Winthrop parents are here—their son was injured only because he'd gone along with the Dupont family for the ride."

"Some ride." She sighed. "Okay. Thanks for filling me in."

Rick tucked his hands in the pockets of his lab coat. "Are you heading back home or do you have an hour to spare?"

"I have time," she said, wondering what he wanted to talk about. Maybe he wanted to give her some friendly advice on how to handle multiple trauma victims in a mini-disaster. Heaven knew, she could use the education.

"Great. I thought maybe we could talk about the goals for the community education committee." He glanced up at the clock on the wall. "We could grab a quick lunch in the cafeteria."

She wasn't very hungry. Emily's condition weighed heavily on her shoulders, but at the same time she didn't want to keep Rick from eating, especially as he was post-call. He looked pretty good for a guy who'd no doubt been up most of the night. "Are you sure you want to do this now? You probably didn't get much sleep last night. We can always talk about the community education plan later."

"Believe it or not, I got about four hours of sleep between four and eight this morning." He led the way out of the conference room, through the PICU and to the elevators. "At this point, I need to stay up or I won't sleep tonight, when I'm supposed to."

She knew what he meant. Being post-call wreaked havoc on a body's sleep cycle. Stepping into the elevator beside him, she caught a whiff of his after-shave and the musky scent filled her head, teasing her pheromones. Her pulse kicked up and she took a subtle step back, hoping the distance would help. He wore a shirt, tie and smart trousers this morning, reminding her of how great he'd looked the night before in a suit, when he'd come in to help her with the MVA victims.

She frowned, a kernel of resentment unfurling in her belly. Wait a minute. She'd given up her chance to become pregnant to help him out. How dared he use the time to go out on a date?

The elevator doors opened and she led the way into the cafeteria, telling herself to drop it. In truth, she was glad to have been there when so many trauma patients had needed her. Even if she had almost caused little Emily more harm than good. Besides, what Rick Weber did in his personal time was none of her business.

Except when he dragged her into it, by asking her to cover his call shift. Maybe she was wrong. Maybe he hadn't been on a date but at something more serious, like a funeral. She helped herself to a salad while Rick went for the barbequed spare ribs. She added a cup of soup to complement her salad, and then stood in line to pay.

"I'll take care of it." Rick spoke up from behind her.

She swallowed another flash of irritation. Would he offer to pay for Chuck's lunch? Or Frank's? Or Dirk's? She highly doubted it.

He must have sensed her mood because he quickly handed a twenty-dollar note to the cashier. "Please. To help pay you back for covering me yesterday."

She arched a brow as they walked to the nearest table. "Don't think you're going to get off that easily. I plan to make you cover one of my call nights in return. Maybe even on a holiday," she threatened.

Rick's laugh was a low, rusty sound and she couldn't help but smile as she sat down opposite him.

"I'm not kidding," she warned.

"I know." He took a bite of his barbequed ribs, not looking too worried.

They ate in silence for a few minutes. When her curiosity got the better of her, she glanced at him. "Should I offer my condolences?"

Startled, he gaped at her. "Why?"

"I thought maybe you attended a funeral, the way you were dressed up when you came in last night." She tried to sound casual, instead of intensely nosy.

"No funeral." Rick stared at his plate for a long moment before meeting her questioning gaze. "I do appreciate you covering for me. I needed to spend time with a very special person."

Her jaw dropped. What nerve! She had been right. He had used her so he could go out on a hot date.

Stabbing the lettuce and tomato in her salad with more force than was necessary, she offered a thin, brittle smile. "Glad you had fun. Who's the lucky woman?"

"Fun might be stretching it a bit," he said with a grimace, seemingly unaware of her ire. "But the lucky woman is Lizzy, my ten-year-old niece. Her father took off right after she was born and she needed a surrogate father to escort her to the father-daughter dance. I know a silly grade-school dance may not seem important to you, but Lizzy means the world to me and I couldn't stand the thought of leaving her to sit at home alone."

His niece? She swallowed hard, ashamed to realize she'd jumped to the wrong conclusion. Not a hot date after all, but family. How could she argue with putting family first? She remembered the father-daughter dance at school. She would have loved to have gone, but her father had been too busy defending a big client at his law firm and hadn't taken time off for such frivolities.

Her stab of resentment faded, replaced by a softening in the region of her heart as she imagined Rick at the dance with a ten-year-old. "I think it's wonderful you cared enough to find cover so you could take your niece to the dance," she said in a low voice. "Lizzy is very lucky to have you."

Their gazes caught, held, and she'd swear every last bit of oxygen had been sucked from her lungs at the steamy intensity of his gaze.

His pager went off and he read the text message. "Ah, excuse me for a moment while I answer this." He rose to his feet and headed for the nearest phone.

She stared at her food, realizing how close she was to making a fool of herself over a man. Again. So what if Rick was sweet, kind, and hotter than burning jet fuel? She'd always avoided dating doctors, her schedule was crazy enough the way it was, and juggling two call schedules was just asking for trouble.

Even her accountant husband hadn't loved her enough to put up with her schedule. Or her infertility. And the few men she'd dated after her divorce hadn't been much better. She'd actually confessed her problems to Denis, but he'd backed off so fast, she'd realized she'd made a huge mistake.

So she'd stopped looking for a relationship. Besides, even if she had been looking for a relationship, Rick was her boss, which meant he was completely off limits. She needed to concentrate on her plans for the future, which included hopefully becoming pregnant and having a baby. A child she'd love with her whole heart.

Not a man.

Rick listened as the resident explained how Tristan Brown, Emily's brother, was insisting on being placed in the same room as his sister. The fact that ICUs didn't have double rooms wasn't a good enough reason. Tristan was insisting on spending the rest of his hospital stay in the parent bed provided in each of the PICU rooms, but there was no way to manage the external fixation device for his open femur fracture on a tiny pull-out bed.

He'd extubated Tristan that morning, and the boy had immediately demanded to know how his sister was doing. Tristan had gotten so agitated, Rick had feared he might need to intubate and sedate him again, in order to prevent more damage to his lower leg fractures. Despite the traction pinning him to the bed, Tristan had threatened to pull himself over to Emily's room, on his elbows if need be.

Rick had believed him.

"I'll be up to see Tristan as soon as I'm finished with lunch," Rick replied. "Emily is still in surgery, getting her Heartmate anyway, so tell Tristan he needs to be patient. We'll have to do some investigating to see if what he's asking for is even possible."

"Will do." The resident hung up the phone.

He returned to the table, taking his seat again.

"So what goals do you envision for the community

education committee?" she asked, pushing her half-eaten salad away.

He tried to bring his attention back to the point of their lunch. "I don't know for sure, but I think we need a few different campaigns."

"There's been quite a bit of press already around drinking and driving, but as eighty percent of our teenage motor vehicle crash patients come in with alcohol in their systems, it's worth repeating."

"Yeah." He knew exactly how Tristan felt. He figured he'd be just as protective with his younger sister, Jess. But at the same time, compromising Tristan's care wasn't an option either.

"Rick? Are you okay?" Naomi asked in concern.

He nodded, realizing he'd been staring down at his half-eaten food. "Yeah. Sorry. Ah, the other big problem we see is that people simply don't pay attention while driving." Gabrielle and Sarah had died in a car crash, they'd been wiped out by some guy who'd run a red light while talking on his cell phone. The guy who'd killed his wife and daughter had been convicted for vehicular homicide, but the knowledge hadn't helped to ease the pain of his loss.

"Cell phones are a menace." Naomi snapped her fingers. "I know we could run some sort of 'Just Drive' campaign. No eating, no make-up, no cell phones. 'Stay Alive, Just Drive' could be our slogan."

"Sounds good." Stay alive, just drive. If only the guy who'd killed Gabrielle and Sarah had done that. His appetite vanished, so he gave up trying to finish his lunch. Just thinking about the accident that had cost his family's lives made him feel ill. He'd thought he could do this, work on something productive to help get over his past, but he'd been wrong. There was no way he could work on this community education campaign after all. "Why don't you see if you can get one of the ED doctors and nurses to help as I'm going to be pretty busy with the whole trauma re-verification process?"

Momentary confusion crossed her features, but she nodded. "Sure. No problem."

"Are you finished?" He suddenly needed to get back to work, to stop fixating on the lingering, ache of his past. "I have to go upstairs to deal with a family issue."

"Yes." She stood when he did and carried her empty tray over to the sideboard. "Is the family issue one of the three from last night?"

"Tristan and Emily Brown." Rick headed toward the elevator. "I extubated Tristan this morning, and now he's insisting on staying in his sister's room. Impossible, considering he has a grade-four liver laceration and a compound fractured femur."

Naomi frowned. "Why is it impossible? Their parents are both patients in the adult unit at Trinity. I can understand why Tristan feels the need to be next to his sister."

He stabbed the button to call the elevator. "I can understand how he feels, too, but that doesn't mean he gets his way. How would we provide care for him? Especially when he's still an ICU patient?"

"I don't know, but I'm sure we could figure out a way." Naomi's chin tilted at a stubborn angle. "Those two kids deserve to be together."

When they entered the unit, there was a team of

medical personnel in Emily's room. The young girl had just come back from surgery.

He followed Naomi in. For several moments they watched from the doorway as the team reconnected her to the bedside heart monitor, the large bulky Heartmate sitting beside her, dwarfing her small, frail frame.

Soon the urgency abated and the number of people in the room dwindled to just the nurse assigned to Emily's care. Rick was about to go and talk to Tristan when he noticed Naomi taking a seat next to Emily's bed.

"Hi, Emily," she whispered, smoothing the young girl's blonde hair away from her face with a tender, caring touch. "Did you know your brother Tristan is here, too? He's right down the hall. He'll be in to visit you very soon. He told me to tell you he loves you. Tristan loves you, Emily." Naomi's voice broke and she blinked away tears. "You're going to feel better soon, you'll see."

His heart lodged in his throat. The compassion on her face tugged at him. He wanted to go to her, to wrap her in his arms and hold her close. Naomi didn't just care about a young patient, this was something more. The wistful expression full of love and caring in her eyes reminded him all too well of the way Gabrielle had looked when she'd held their daughter in her arms.

He shook his head. What was wrong with him? He shouldn't be attracted to Naomi, especially not when in that fleeting moment the keen compassion in her eyes had reminded him of his wife.

Gabrielle and Sarah deserved better than to be shoved aside and forgotten.

He turned away, tearing his gaze from Naomi. Somehow, some way, he had to find a way to keep the pretty surgeon at a safe distance. So she didn't threaten his sanity.

CHAPTER FOUR

NAOMI returned to the hospital at five o'clock that evening to start her overnight call shift. When she arrived in the PICU, Rick didn't smile but gave her a reserved nod.

"Ready to make rounds?" he asked.

"Sure." She frowned as they walked toward the first patient's room, sending him a sidelong glance. Had she done something to make him angry?

"Justin Wright has a sixteen-year-old gunshot wound to the belly and was admitted the night before last, on Debra's shift." Rick's voice was devoid of all emotion—he could have been reciting from an encyclopedia rather than describing a patient's condition. "He's running a fever so I switched his antibiotics this morning. If he doesn't improve, he may need to go back to surgery to have his abdomen explored."

"All right." She made a notation on her sheet. They moved down to the next patient's room. He continued talking in that same monotone voice, describing the current treatment regime for Jimmy and Chelsey Dupont, two of the patients she'd admitted the night before. As they made their way through the unit, Rick's demeanor never changed. It was as if the moments they had spent together during last night's crisis and their earlier lunch had never happened.

She reminded herself it was for the best. Rick was her boss. A professional relationship was the only thing they could ever share. Hadn't she learned her lesson with Andrew?

Men wanted more than she could give.

Rick paused outside Tristan's doorway. The teen was agitated, his sheets tangled around his limbs, his heart rate tipping over one hundred. His left femur with the open fracture was suspended from the traction pole above his bed, and she didn't like the way he twisted and turned, as if trying to get away.

"Has he had any sedation?" Rick asked Angie, the nurse on duty.

"I've given him ten milligrams of morphine and another five of Versed over the past hour, but it hasn't touched him." Angie appeared flustered and a tad disgruntled, no doubt from the hours she'd spent wrestling with her patient.

"Don't you think he'd be better off if we could find a way to bunk him in Emily's room?" Naomi asked, glancing up at Rick.

"No. He's better off here, where he can care for him properly." Rick increased the orders for Tristan's sedation and then moved on to the next patient.

Frowning, she followed him to the next bedside. When they arrived at Emily's room a few minutes later, she was glad to see the young girl was doing a little better. Granted, she was still on vasopressors to keep her blood pressure up, and her lungs needed the support of a ventilator, not to mention the Heartmate doing the work of her heart, but, as critical as Emily had been, Naomi chose to celebrate the smaller signs of improvement. Her labs had stabilized and they were edging downward on her blood-pressure medication.

"Any questions?" Rick asked with a raised brow, making her realize Emily was the last patient.

"No. I think you've covered everything."

"See you tomorrow." Rick moved away, barely giving her a backward glance.

What on earth had happened since she'd left after lunch to run a few errands? She didn't know and shouldn't care quite so much. Shrugging off his indifference, she went back to Tristan's room to see if she could help calm the boy down.

"Tristan? I just spoke to Emily. I told her how much you loved her." She rested a soothing hand on his shoulder. "Please, don't hurt yourself any more. You need to get better, to heal so you can see Emily."

His fevered gaze locked on hers. "She's okay? Em is okay?"

"She's doing better, I promise." She breathed a sigh of relief when Tristan stopped struggling. "Rest now, and we'll work on arranging another visit—all right?"

He nodded, his eyelids drooping with exhaustion. He was still pretty banged up himself and needed to be watched closely for internal bleeding. If he kept thrashing around the bed like a wild man, he risked causing more tissue damage to his liver laceration.

"Keep him as quiet as possible," Naomi said to Angie. "Maybe the medication will finally kick in."

"I hope so." Angie hesitated, and then asked, "Dr Horton? I know it's highly unusual, but what if we used a smaller toddler bed for Emily and made room for Tristan's bed next to hers? He doesn't really need all that much care, other than the traction and to keep a close eye on his vital signs."

"I know. But how would we monitor his vitals? The rooms aren't set up to have two patients, there aren't two bedside monitors." Naomi studied Tristan's bed and then pictured the already crowded room of his sister. "Emily's Heartmate takes up quite a bit of room, too. I'm not sure we can work around two beds crammed into one room."

"You're probably right." Angie frowned. "I just wish there was something I could do. No adults have been in to visit either of them today. The parents are both patients in the ICU at Trinity, but what about aunts and uncles? Or grandparents? I can't believe there hasn't been a single person here. It's a shame they can't be together."

Naomi couldn't help but agree. She moved away from Tristan's bedside and made her way down to see Justin Wright, the teen with the fever. His temperature was stable, so she didn't need to do anything more.

Emily was fine, her care managed by the cardiothoracic surgeons, but the trauma team was on the case as a consult. Standing in Emily's room, she realized if they took the sleeper chair out, moved the Heartmate to the other side of the bed and put Emily in the smaller-sized toddler bed, there would be room for her brother.

But no way to monitor his vital signs.

She turned away to finish reviewing the rest of her patients' charts. Stopping by Mike Winthrop's room, she saw both of his parents sitting side by side, their arms wrapped around each other as they gazed down at their sleeping son.

The sight made her pause. Mike's mother had obviously been weeping, but his father was there for her to hang onto. Even though Mike's father wasn't crying, she suspected he appreciated leaning on his wife, too. Mike's injury was relatively serious, his pelvic fracture meaning that he'd need a temporary colostomy and possibly a urinary catheter for a long time.

A flicker of doubt caught her off guard. Maybe her decision to raise a baby alone wasn't the best after all. If something happened to her child, she wouldn't have anyone else to lean on.

She was strong, she wouldn't have made it through the male-dominated world of trauma surgery if she wasn't, yet there was no feeling more helpless than that of a parent watching his or her child suffer. She swallowed hard and turned away.

There were single parents all over the world, and they managed. Yet, truthfully, most of them hadn't planned to be single parents. When a spouse died, there wasn't a whole lot of choice about whether or not to raise your child alone. So did that mean single parents did a worse job than two parents? No, she refused to believe it.

She pressed a hand over her flat belly. She'd lost her baby so early, she'd never felt the baby move. Hadn't seen any outward sign of the new life she'd carried so briefly. Not until the cramping pain had gripped her lower abdomen and the bleeding had begun.

Closing her eyes, she remembered the helplessness, the horrified realization that she was losing her baby and there was nothing she could do to stop it.

"Dr Horton?" Carrie, one of the nurses, pulled her back to the present. "Would you come and look at this patient's incision for me?"

"Of course." She shook off her memories of the past and followed Carrie into the patient's room. She looked at the incision, didn't like the way it was healing and changed the treatment plan accordingly. She did one more run-through of the unit, and went down to grab a quick sandwich in the cafeteria.

Hiding a yawn, she debated what to do next. It was still early, barely eight-thirty, but everything was calm for the moment. She had her pager on, so there was no need for her to wander down to the E.D. to see if anything was happening. They'd page if they heard of any patients on their way in.

She grabbed a pair of scrubs out of the O.R. locker room before heading down to the lower level on-call rooms. After changing her clothes, she stretched out on the bed for a short nap, having learned during her training to take advantage of every moment of sleep.

Her short nap extended to almost two hours. When her pager went off, she nearly shot out of bed, momentarily disoriented. She turned on the small bedside light and peered down at her pager.

Not a trauma call, but one of the nurses in the PICU. She reached for the phone. "This is Naomi. Did someone page me?"

"Naomi, it's Angie. I need your help with Tristan Brown. I thought he was sleeping when suddenly his monitor started to triple-beep. I ran into the room and found him more than halfway out of bed. He'd almost pulled his fractured leg completely out of the traction sling. He's insisting on seeing his sister. What should I do?"

Naomi sighed. "Unless you can come up with a way to install two bedside monitors in Emily's room, I don't think there's anything we can do. His condition is too tenuous to bypass continuous vital-sign monitoring."

There was a moment of silence on the other end of the phone. "What if I can come up with an option for that? Will you consider putting them together into one room?"

"Yes. I'll be right up." Naomi hung up and made a quick stop in the bathroom before heading upstairs to the PICU.

She found Angie and Doreen in Emily's room, moving equipment around. She put her hands on her hips and surveyed the results. "That's exactly what I would have done, but what about the second bedside monitor?"

"I called our biomedical tech and he agreed to come in and install Tristan's monitor here on a portable bedside stand." Angie bit her lip nervously. "We'll need to keep a close eye on it, but there's always someone in Emily's room anyway, as she's sick enough to warrant having her own nurse."

Oh, boy. It worked, but they were absolutely stretching the rules. "Do you think we need to call Joan at home about this?" Joan Cranberg was the nurse manager of the PICU.

Angie looked embarrassed. "I already did. Honestly, I really believe it's in Tristan's best interests to be moved into his sister's room. He's going to hurt himself if we don't."

"Yeah, and I can't stand the thought of poor Emily not having any visitors," Doreen added. "We always joke about not allowing any bunk beds, but this is an exceptional case."

Naomi blew out a breath, wondering what Rick would say when he walked in. Yet she was the attending physician of record, and she agreed with Angie. Moving Tristan was for the best, at least for tonight. If things didn't work out as well as they hoped, there was no reason they couldn't move him back.

"All right, let's get Tristan moved."

Doreen and Angie broke into wide grins. "We have almost everything ready. All we need is for the biomed tech to show up."

He arrived a few minutes later. It turned out that they didn't need to move Tristan's bedside monitor but could use a portable spare that Biomed had down in their shop. Less than half an hour later, they had Tristan safely installed in Emily's room.

"We can't admit anyone to Tristan's empty bed," she informed Angie. "This is still officially his room number. None of the computer systems are going to allow two patients in one room. As far as the hospital system knows, he's still in his old room."

"I know." Angie watched Tristan as he gazed at his

sister. "But just look at him. See how calm he is? I really think this is going to work."

"I hope so." She didn't want to think about what Rick would say if something bad happened. Yet Tristan's serene expression was reassuring. "I really hope so."

Rick woke up feeling groggy and not very well rested. Naomi had invaded his dreams, making him toss and turn restlessly throughout the night, until his hard, aching body dragged him from sleep.

He rested his head in his hands, realizing on a dour note that celibacy might not be in his best interests. Two years since Gabrielle and Sarah had died and he hadn't touched another woman. Hadn't wanted to.

Until now.

He'd tried to keep his distance from Naomi as they'd made rounds, but it had been harder than he'd imagined. Especially when she'd kept sending him puzzled glances, as if trying to figure out why he was angry or upset. After he'd handed over the care of their patients, he'd left as quickly as he could, but it hadn't mattered much, because she'd followed him into his dreams.

After taking a quick and very cold shower, Rick decided to head into work. He wasn't on call today, but as Chief of Trauma Surgery he happened to have a couple of medical executive staff meetings to attend. Before that, though, he wanted to see how his ICU patients were doing.

Driving to the hospital, he hoped Naomi's night

hadn't been too rough. He picked up a steaming cup of coffee and sipped the brew on his way to the PICU.

The first bedside he visited was Tristan's. His heart nearly stopped in his chest when he saw the room was empty. Tristan's name was still printed outside the door, but where was the patient? Had something happened during the night? Had Naomi been forced to take him to the O.R. for some reason?

"Hi, Rick. Are you looking for Tristan? He's in Emily's room."

"Emily's room?" Scowling, he marched down the hall to Emily's room, annoyed that Naomi had gone directly against his orders. When he reached Emily's doorway he stopped and stared.

Tristan was lying on his own bed, his right arm extended out across the beds so he could hold his sister's hand. Emily was resting quietly beside him. Tristan was connected to a portable monitor on a table next to his bed. Dumbfounded, Rick reached out to pick up Tristan's clipboard. The boy hadn't taken anything for pain or sedation for the past six hours. Yet he was certainly resting quietly.

Amazing. Naomi had been right. All the boy had needed was to be close to his young sister.

His anger faded. Naomi had covered all the bases— what more could he could say? Except maybe apologize for not listening to her in the first place.

His pager went off, announcing the arrival of a eight-year-old boy struck by a car while riding his bicycle. As he hadn't seen any other trauma surgeons around, he headed downstairs to the E.D.

Naomi was there, waiting for the patient. Her shift

had officially ended at eight a.m. and Frank should have been there to relieve her by now.

"Where's Frank Turner?" he asked when he saw her.

"He'll be here by ten." Naomi eyed him warily. "Have you been up to the unit yet?"

"Yeah." Before he could say anything more, their patient arrived.

"Eight-year-old with closed cranial trauma and fractured left femur." The paramedics rattled off the boy's vital signs. "He's not responding to verbal stimuli and his pupils are unequal, right larger than the left."

"Call Radiology. We'll need to get a head CT scan stat." Naomi took charge of the situation, as if he wasn't there. He was amazed at how she handled a trauma scene, despite only having had a couple of years' experience. "Don't go crazy with the fluids until we know the extent of his head injury."

"No helmet?" Rick frowned at the gash across the kid's forehead.

"No." Naomi's tone was grim. "There's no way to know if the parents didn't enforce the rule or if he just didn't listen."

Either scenario was possible. He watched as Naomi did her physical examination, making sure there were no other hidden injures. When she'd finished, she stepped back. "Get him into the scanner and then take him directly upstairs to the PICU. I want those CT results asap."

The nurse nodded and wheeled the boy away.

"Shouldn't you be sleeping?" Rick asked.

She lifted a brow. "I got five hours of sleep last night, an hour more than you did the night before."

"Right." He couldn't argue against himself. "Doesn't mean you have to hang around here. I can cover until Frank gets here."

"I thought you had meetings?"

He shrugged. "Good reason to skip them. Patient care comes first."

She laughed and his breath caught in his throat. Damn, she was beautiful. Smart. Sexy. And dangerous. Very dangerous. Her eyes twinkled and she held up a hand. "No way. I'll stay, you go to your high-powered meetings. I don't have anything else to rush off for anyway."

He found that somewhat hard to believe. What did Naomi do in her free time? Was there someone special in her life? A man? For all he knew, his secret lust could be for a woman who was already in a relationship. She'd broken her plans to cover him the other night. What sort of plans? The stab of jealousy pierced deep.

"I'm sorry." The apology came out rather abruptly.

She glanced at him in surprise. "For what?"

"For not listening to you about Tristan."

"Oh." She gave him a tentative smile. "I guess that means you already know we moved him into Emily's room. Angie called me around midnight because he'd almost crawled out of bed to get to his sister. Don't be upset, I had to move him."

"I'm not upset." He stuffed his hands into his pockets to prevent himself reaching out to her. There was so much he wanted to say, but the words lodged in his throat. They were standing in the middle of the ED, so this wasn't exactly the time or place to bare his soul.

"Would you be willing to meet me for dinner later?" he blurted out the invitation before he could think about the ramifications. "Unless, of course, you already have plans."

"I— Uh, no plans." Naomi couldn't have looked more shocked, but she nodded. "Sure. I can meet you for dinner."

Relief flooded him. "Good. I'll give you a call later, if that's all right."

"I'll be at home."

His pager went off again, but this time it was one of his colleagues, not a trauma call or the PICU. "I have to go. I'll see you later."

He spun on his heel and headed for the nearest phone. There was a pediatric trauma patient up in the Fox Valley who needed to be transferred down for better care. He gave his opinion to the ortho surgeon who'd received the original call, and they agreed to transfer the patient. He hung up, glad to have the issue resolved.

When he turned back, Naomi was gone. The tiny light inside him faded a little, but he told himself it didn't matter because he'd be seeing her that evening.

Dinner. He should have felt guilty, but he didn't. Instead, he looked forward to seeing Naomi again.

CHAPTER FIVE

NAOMI didn't leave the hospital but went back up to the PICU to see Tomas, the eight-year-old boy who'd been riding his bike when he'd been struck by a car. She was very worried about the severity of his head injury.

Tomas had just arrived in the PICU from the CT scanner. Her pager went off with the radiology phone number a second later. Fearful of the results, she picked up the phone. "Naomi Horton."

"Tomas Parnell's head CT doesn't look good. He has a bad shearing injury and diffuse areas of brain swelling. You'll need to be very aggressive with his treatment. And even then, the likelihood of survival is slim."

Poor prognosis. Dear God. He was only eight years old. She rubbed a hand over her brow, feeling slightly sick. "Thanks for letting me know." She called the operator and requested that Neurosurgery be paged stat. This boy needed every possible chance if he was going to survive.

"Put him on the hypothermia protocol," she told Glenn, the PICU nurse. "I want you to hit him with a dose of Lasix and mannitol, too."

Glenn nodded and went to work. The neurosurgeon, a man by the name of Cliff Baker, arrived and she explained about Tomas's CT scan. Cliff walked over to the nearest radiology computer and looked at the films himself. "Yeah, it's not good. A shearing injury is where one part of the brain goes one way, and the rest of the brain goes another. The kid must have flown pretty far through the air before he hit the ground. I'll put an intracranial probe in place, so we can measure his intracranial pressure."

"Thanks." Placing ICP monitors was the neurosurgeon's area of expertise, so she simply sat at Tomas's bedside. As his mother wasn't there yet, she took the young boy's hand in hers and talked to him. "Tomas, your mother is on her way. She loves you very much." His face was so innocent, with hardly a mark on him other than the gash on his forehead, that no one would never know his brain was damaged so severely. Her heart ached for the potential loss of a young life.

"Naomi?" She glanced up to see Rick standing in the doorway. "Do you have a minute?"

"Sure." She came out of Tomas's room, frowning at the serious expression on his face. "What's wrong?"

"Frank's wife called me. He won't be in to cover his shift, because he's been admitted to Trinity Medical Center."

"Admitted?" She sucked in a breath. "What happened?"

"He thought the discomfort in his chest was indigestion, but it turns out he's having an acute myocardial infarction." Rick's expression was grim. "They're talking about trying a coronary artery stent first, but he may need surgery."

"Oh, no," she whispered. "Poor Frank."

"I'm going to cover the daytime shift, Debra has agreed to cover his call for tonight." Rick glanced around the unit. "If you wouldn't mind filling me in on anything in particular that happened last night."

Of course she didn't mind, but before she could start, there was a commotion from the other end of the hall.

"Tomas? Where's my baby?" a hysterical female voice cried out, interrupting them. "Where's my son?"

Naomi hurried over, putting a comforting arm around the woman's shoulders. "I'm Dr Horton, and your son is right here." She steered the crying woman into Tomas's room, glad the ICP monitor had already been placed so the woman could go straight in.

"Tomas? Oh, my gosh, look at him. What are all those tubes? He's not awake. Can he hear me? Is he going to be okay?" Mrs Parnell grabbed his hand, but her gaze clung to Naomi's. "Is my baby going to be okay?"

She hated this part of her job. Feeling close to tears herself, she stepped closer. "I don't know. Tomas has a very bad head injury. We're going to do everything we can for him, but right now his brain is swelling in response to the tissue damage, the same sort of swelling you get with a hurt ankle or wrist."

"Oh, no, no, no." Tomas's mother broke down, sobbing.

"Hopefully we'll get the swelling under control." She didn't want to explain how the blood flow to his head would be cut off if they couldn't. "Please, believe me, we're doing everything possible to help him."

His mother nodded, but was still clutching Tomas's hand and crying. Naomi stood next to her for a few minutes, trying to offer comfort, wishing there was something more she could do. "Do you have anyone I can call to come be with you?" she asked. "A friend or a relative?"

"No." She shook her head, struggling to get her crying under control. "My husband is on his way home—he's in Dallas. My parents live in Florida."

Naomi looked at Tomas's ICP reading on the bedside monitor. The numbers were already creeping up. If they got too high, when the pressure in his head became higher than his blood pressure, they were in serious trouble. "Call them," she advised. "Call your parents, have them come up."

Tomas's mother turned pale, but she nodded. "I will."

Naomi stayed for a few minutes longer, and then turned to find Rick. He was standing outside Tomas's room, a strange expression on his face. "Rick? Are you all right?"

He acted as if he hadn't heard her, his gaze locked on Tomas and his mother.

"Rick?" Concerned, she took his arm and steered him away, half dragging him toward the physician conference room. There were a few residents in there and when she jerked her head toward the door, they took her unspoken request to heart and vanished. "Rick, what's wrong?"

"I—I just…" His voice trailed off and he shook his

head, without finishing his sentence. He walked to the window, staring blindly out at the parking lot.

She couldn't help feeling as if something about Tomas's case had hit him on a personal level. She didn't know anything about his private life prior to coming to Milwaukee. Had he lost someone close to him? A child?

"Rick, I'm here if you need to talk." She kept her voice low, soothing. Although he stood with his back toward her, she went over to stand beside him, putting her hand on his arm. "Any time."

"I'm fine." His gruff voice betrayed his inner turmoil.

"You don't look fine," Naomi gently argued. "In fact, you were staring at Tomas as if you were seeing a ghost."

He closed his eyes and rested his forehead against the glass. "Yeah," he admitted softly. "Maybe I was."

She didn't feel any satisfaction in knowing her instincts were right. Prying wasn't something she wanted to do, yet it was clear something was bothering him. He probably needed to talk. "Whose ghost? If you want to tell me."

He opened his eyes and turned from the window, his expression bleak. "My daughter. Sometimes, when I look at a very sick child, especially one that might be heading for brain death, I can only see my daughter, Sarah."

Stunned speechless, she stared at him. "I'm sorry. I didn't know you had a daughter."

"She was so sweet, so innocent." Rick's tortured expression sliced her heart. "For two days I stayed at her bedside, but she died. Her brain swelled too much. They couldn't save her."

Dear God, how horrible. Naomi acted on instinct, sliding her arms around Rick's waist and giving him a comforting hug. "I'm sorry, Rick. I'm so sorry."

He stayed as stiff as a board for a moment, and she was just about to pull away when he wrapped his arms around her and held her close. "I loved her, loved Sarah and Gabrielle," he murmured. "And I lost them both."

Gabrielle must have been his wife. He'd lost his wife and his daughter. She didn't know what to say, so she simply held him, offering what meager comfort she could.

Abruptly he pulled away, as if the moment of weakness had never happened. "Sorry. I shouldn't let it get to me like that."

"You don't have to apologize." Helplessly, she watched him, wishing there was more she could do. "Losing your wife and daughter must have been horrible."

"Doesn't matter." The in-control surgeon was back. "I don't let it interfere with my work."

How he managed to continue to take care of peds trauma patients after losing his daughter, she'd never know.

"Thanks." He turned to stare at her.

"Any time." Their brief embrace hadn't been at all sexual, simply friendly and comforting. Yet the longer he stared at her, the more the atmosphere subtly changed. They weren't even touching, but she felt almost as if they were, the way the room shrank around them.

Annoyed with herself for noticing, especially when he was obviously still very much in love with his dead wife, she took a step towards the door. Then she turned back and almost walked right into him.

He grasped her arms. For a moment she felt as if she couldn't breathe, and then he surprised her by reaching up to touch her face. Then lowering his mouth to hers.

His kiss wasn't a soft, gentle gesture of appreciation, as she'd expected. Instead, his mouth was hot, greedy and took possession of hers without asking.

She couldn't help but respond, accepting his kiss, taking everything he had to offer and wanting more. He tasted wonderful, like brandy-flavored coffee with a hint of cinnamon. When he gently tugged her closer, she ignored the warning bleeps in the back of her mind and reveled in the embrace.

Her pager went off, vibrating like mad at her waist. She broke off the kiss, breathing heavily, as she fumbled for it.

Not a trauma call, thank heavens, but she didn't recognize the phone number. She glanced up at Rick, who seemed embarrassed and possibly grateful for the interruption. "I'd better answer this."

"I know." His blue eyes had turned distant and he stepped around her, taking several steps toward the door. "I'll, uh, be out here when you're ready to report off on the patients."

She bit her lip in dismay, knowing she needed to be strong and brush off the electrifying effect of his kiss. Reaching for the phone, she nodded. "Sure. I'll meet you in a few minutes."

The call wasn't urgent, so she gave an order to

increase a patient's dose of pain medication and hung up. She stood for a moment in the empty conference room, willing her heart rate to return to normal.

Rick was her boss. That heated kiss shouldn't have happened. Her head knew the situation was impossible. Even if she wasn't his subordinate, his grief over his dead wife and child was totally heart-wrenching. And she wasn't an idiot. The last thing she needed was to be some guy's rebound romance.

She rested a hand over her flat, barren stomach. She didn't have a future to offer any man. Even if he was interested, what would Rick say if he knew the likelihood of her becoming pregnant was slim? Her doctor had warned her how much scar tissue she had in her Fallopian tubes from endometriosis.

Swallowing hard, she straightened her shoulders and told herself to get over it. She needed to walk through the unit with Rick, give him an update on the care of their patients, and then go home.

It wasn't until they were halfway through rounds that she remembered their tentative plans to share dinner.

Rick tried to concentrate on what Naomi was telling him, but it wasn't easy. Her scent clung to his clothes, seeming to cloud every breath, filling his brain.

He shouldn't have kissed her. Not that he thought she'd file some sort of sexual harassment claim or anything, but the possibility was enough to remind him how inappropriate his behavior had been.

He wasn't even sure how it had happened. One

minute she had been walking away and the next she had practically been in his arms.

Drawing in a deep breath, he tried to shake the nagging guilt. Gabrielle was gone, there was no reason he couldn't kiss another woman, yet the feeling was there all the same. He'd missed his wife and his daughter, but he'd kissed Naomi.

And what did that say about him? Nothing good.

Naomi was a warm, generous person. He'd watched her comfort Tomas's distraught mother. She would have done the same for him, almost had if he hadn't found a way to pull himself together.

She'd cared about him like a friend. Why had he taken something so sweet and turned it into edgy desire?

He didn't know, but couldn't deny he'd do it again if given half a chance.

"I think we've covered everyone," she said, avoiding his gaze. "Any questions? If not, I think I'll head home."

He pulled himself together. "No questions. Thanks for staying late to fill the early part of Frank's shift."

"Of course." She frowned. "I should probably call his wife, see how things are going."

"I told her to page me if he needed surgery." He didn't like the awkwardness between them and mentally kicked himself for crossing the line. "I'd be happy to let you know if something changes."

"Sounds good." Naomi finally brought her eyes to meet his, but he couldn't tell what was going on in her mind. The way she'd responded to his kiss didn't give him the impression she was angry, even though she had every right to be. Her smile didn't reach her eyes when she added, "Let me know if you need anything."

He needed her, but luckily managed to bite his tongue before admitting that out loud. "I will."

She turned and walked away. He deliberately didn't let himself watch her exit. The kiss shouldn't have happened, or at least it shouldn't have gotten out of control.

He took a call about a new admission, the young boy being transferred from the hospital in the Fox Valley. Ortho had accepted the patient but they wanted a trauma consult.

The child wasn't sick enough to be in the PICU, so Rick went out to the general floor to examine him. He concurred with the ortho surgeon's assessment and agreed to help keep an eye on the boy, whose name was Roscoe.

Jess paged him about an hour later. When he called her back, she invited him over for dinner that evening.

"Lizzy is making dinner to earn her cooking girl scout badge and she wants you to come over."

Dinner. Damn. Hadn't he asked Naomi to go out to dinner with him? He mentally slapped himself in the head. Not a smart move. Especially after that kiss. "I don't know, Jess, I think I already have a date."

"You think you have a date?" The laughter mixed with excitement in his sister's voice was unmistakable. "Awesome. Who are you going out with? Is she pretty? Anyone I know?"

"No one you know." He sighed and rubbed the back of his neck. How would Naomi feel if he cancelled?

Had she even remembered their tentative plans? They had been made before he'd known about Frank.

Before their kiss.

Coward, he berated himself. He couldn't stand Naomi up or make up some excuse to get out of their plans. Maybe they needed to have this dinner so they could talk about what had happened. He could reassure her that he wouldn't cross the line again.

The thought of facing Naomi and having a serious conversation about what had happened or, worse, telling her they had no future made his stomach twist into a big, hard knot.

"Why don't you bring her along?" Jess suggested, blithely unaware of his internal chaos. "I'd love to meet her."

"Jess," he warned. "Don't. She's just a friend, all right? She's one of the trauma surgeons on staff here, and I don't want you making more out of this than there is."

"Who, me?" His sister's tone was deceptively innocent. "I wouldn't think of it."

He couldn't say no to Lizzy's cooking, so he agreed. "I'll ask her, but don't be surprised if she refuses and politely backs out of the invite."

"I bet she won't. And if you'd rather just go out for a romantic meal alone, that's fine with me, too. I know Lizzy will understand." Jess sounded positively cheerful as she hung up.

He closed his cell phone and stared at it for a long moment. He needed to call Naomi. To explain how he'd forgotten about dinner plans with his sister and

Lizzy but that she was more than welcome to come along.

Would she decline the invitation? What in the world had he been thinking to invite her out in the first place? There were rules about superiors dating subordinates, he knew them just as well as Naomi did. Yet he'd deluded himself into thinking there was no harm in the two of them sharing a meal and getting to know each other better.

Of course, that had been before he'd practically jumped her in the physician conference room. Cripes, who was he kidding? His physical response to Naomi was anything but innocent.

He opened his phone and scrolled through the trauma team's numbers, which he'd entered during his first day on the job. His having their numbers was legitimate, because he needed to be able to get in touch with any of them at any time.

Naomi's was lost in the middle of the list, as they were in alphabetical order. He dialed in her number and waited for her to answer.

"Hello?"

Just hearing her husky voice made his pulse race. "Naomi? We didn't finalize our plans for dinner tonight, but would you mind going over to my sister's house? Lizzy needs to make a full meal in order to get her cooking girl scout badge."

There was a short silence and he found himself gripping his phone tightly. Had she changed her mind, then? He couldn't blame her if she had. It would be the smart move for both of them.

Too bad he wasn't feeling so smart.

"Sure," she said finally. "I'd love to meet your sister and your niece."

"Are you certain?" he asked, worried she wasn't too thrilled with the change of plans. "I'm sure Lizzy will understand if you want to go someplace else."

"No, don't disappoint her," Naomi protested quickly. "I'm sure. I'll meet you at the hospital at six."

CHAPTER SIX

Rick wasn't surprised when Naomi arrived promptly. He noticed she was always on time for her shifts, too. He insisted on driving over and she grilled him on the patients as they rode to his sister's.

"Tomas is hanging in there, his ICPs are still in the low teens." Taking care of the severely brain-injured boy wasn't easy, he was glad the neurosurgeons were co-managing the boy's care. "Tristan is doing great, he's much better in Emily's room. He's probably ready to go to a regular floor, but the nurses all want him to stay in the unit with Emily."

"I'm sure it's best for both of them," Naomi agreed. "Is Emily doing better?"

"Yeah, her vital signs are good and she's off her blood-pressure medication." He'd stood in Emily's room and could have sworn the young girl knew her brother was lying next to her. He had to believe the two of them would get better if they stayed together.

He pulled up in front of his sister's house, shooting a quick glance at Naomi. She wore slim black pants and a cranberry-red blouse. With her dark hair and creamy skin, she looked stunning.

Why hadn't some guy already snapped her up? he wondered as they walked up to the front door. Surely the men in the hospital weren't blind or stupid. He was all too aware of her warm scent as she stood beside him.

Before he could knock, Lizzy opened the door to let them inside.

"Something smells good," he said, as he gave his niece a hug.

"I made lasagna and homemade garlic bread," Lizzy announced proudly. "And chocolate brownies for dessert."

"Yum," Naomi said. "Sounds delicious."

"A meal worth a cooking badge," he agreed. When his sister walked in, he quickly introduced Naomi. "Naomi, my sister Jessica and her daughter Elizabeth. Jess, Lizzy, this is Naomi Horton."

"Uncle Rick, nobody calls me Elizabeth," Lizzy protested. "Nice to meet you, Naomi."

"Nice to meet you, too. I heard you had a great time at the father-daughter dance."

"It was the most fun ever!" Lizzy jumped up and began flapping her arms like a bird. "We did the chicken dance."

"Really?" Naomi raised a brow and glanced at him while he grimaced. "I have like to have seen that."

Yeah, over his dead body. "No, you wouldn't."

"Uncle Rick isn't a very good dancer," Lizzy confided to Naomi as they walked into the kitchen. "We were the first group cut out of the dance contest."

"Bummer," Naomi said with a mock frown. "Maybe he needs some lessons."

Lizzy's eyes sparkled. "Yeah, maybe."

Jess arched a brow. "Lizzy, you'd better check your garlic bread."

Lizzy's mouth dropped open and she flew over to the oven, carefully using the large oven mitts to protect her hands when she pulled the bread out. "Whew. It's not burned."

Rick grinned. "You're lucky. That's what you get for making cracks about my dancing."

Naomi seemed to enjoy herself, although she treated him as if they were nothing more than friends. He was disappointed even though he told himself not to be. Wasn't that the whole purpose for bringing Naomi to Jess's house for dinner, rather than a romantic, intimate meal in a fancy restaurant? To dilute the sensual effect of their kiss?

Too bad it wasn't working. He'd kiss her again if he could.

"Lizzy, your lasagna is excellent," Naomi declared. "Good enough to earn two merit badges."

"Thanks." Lizzy's eyes glowed from the compliment. Rick could tell Jess and Lizzy both liked Naomi. The conversation flowed from one topic to the other without difficulty.

"Uncle Rick, will you help me with my math homework?" Lizzy asked when they were finished.

"Yes, will you, please?" Jess added with an imploring gaze. "I swear her fourth-grade math is already over my head."

How could he refuse? "Sure thing."

"I'll help with the dishes," Naomi said, jumping to her feet and grabbing plates to clear the table.

"Let's leave them to their math," Jess agreed, following Naomi into the kitchen.

Rick helped Lizzy decipher her math problem. "Do you understand it now?" he asked.

"I think so." Her small brow was furrowed.

"Why don't you try the next one while I get us some refills on lemonade?"

Lizzy nodded, chewing on the end of her pen as she read the next problem. As he moved toward the doorway, he overheard the conversation in the kitchen.

"Does Lizzy ever see her dad?"

"No, he disappeared shortly after she was born." Jess didn't sound bitter, just matter-of-fact.

"I'm sure that's been hard for both of you." Naomi's voice held a note of empathy.

"Yeah, at times, like when there's a father-daughter dance at school." Jess sighed. "Most of the time it's not so bad, although I'm sure when Lizzy hits her teenage years I'll wish I had someone to help."

There was a pause as they washed and dried some dishes. "Jess, do you mind if I ask you a personal question?"

"Not at all."

Rick found himself leaning forward to hear Naomi's question. "If you had to do it all over again, give birth to Lizzy, knowing her father wouldn't be around to help, would you still do it? Or would you make a different decision?"

"Yes." There wasn't a moment's hesitation on his Jess's part. "Absolutely." A dreamy expression softened her. "Lizzy is my life. I can't imagine not having her with me. I don't regret one minute of our time together."

Naomi's tone was wistful. "That's what I thought. She's a great kid. You're very lucky."

"I know."

"I can only hope I can have a family some day."

Naomi's words stopped him cold. She wanted a family, like most women did. He shouldn't have been surprised. Feeling awkward, he cleared his throat, warning them he was coming in. "Hey, Lizzy wants more lemonade."

"I bet you do, too." Jess refilled both glasses. "Have you finished her math? I swear I'm going to need a full-time tutor for her soon. I'm so clueless."

"Almost finished," he promised. He glanced at Naomi, who was pretty much ignoring him.

He headed into the dining room, carrying the two glasses of lemonade. Lizzy had done two more problems but was having trouble on the last one. He helped her set it up and she took it from there.

"Brownies?" Jess asked, carrying in a heaped plate of Lizzy's treat.

"Yay, I'm finished." Lizzy slammed her math book closed. She eagerly reached for a brownie. "They're good." Lizzy almost sounded surprised.

They left after they'd finished dessert. Naomi was uncharacteristically quiet as he drove back to the hospital.

"Your sister is very nice. I'm glad I got to meet her," she said finally.

He smiled. "Jess liked you, too."

"She makes being a single mom look easy."

His smile faded. "It's not easy, but I'm here now and help out as much as I can. Jess won't be raising Lizzy completely on her own. I'm here to do whatever is necessary."

There was a long, awkward silence.

"Naomi—" he started.

"Rick—" she said at the same time. Then she waved a hand at him. "Go ahead."

He swallowed hard. "As your boss, I need to apologize for the way I kissed you."

She pursed her lips. "And if you weren't my boss?"

Damn. She would ask that. Especially now that he knew what she wanted out of life. Still, he couldn't lie. "I'd want to kiss you again, even though I don't have anything more to offer you."

"I see." She frowned a bit. "Nothing to offer? I assume you mean no future, just a moment of pleasure."

It didn't sound good when she said it out loud. "I don't think I can go down that path again," he admitted. "Although you're the only one who's ever tempted me in the past two years."

Her smile was sad. "I'm flattered, but I don't do flings."

"I know." He pulled up to the hospital and kept the engine idling. "I'm sorry."

"Don't be. You're a nice guy, Rick." She opened her door and stepped out. "Take care," she added.

"You too."

She closed the door and walked into the hospital. He suspected she'd go up and check on the PICU patients before going home.

He clenched the steering wheel and had to talk himself out of following her. She wanted a family. Naomi didn't do flings. He wasn't looking for anything more. They needed to maintain a professional relationship.

Leaving Naomi and driving home alone wasn't easy. But if leaving her after just sharing a kiss hadn't been easy, he knew for sure he'd be doomed if he allowed things to go further.

He pushed her firmly out of his mind, but once again, later that night, she crept back into his dreams.

Naomi woke up the next morning feeling groggy. It was Saturday and she was off work for the whole day. And even better, she didn't have to go back into the hospital until Sunday morning.

A whole day with nothing to do. She folded her hands behind her head and debated how to spend her day. She hadn't done any shopping for a while, although to be honest it wasn't her favorite pastime. She should probably hit the gym, she hadn't worked out for weeks.

Or maybe she should at least stop in at the hospital to check on Tomas. Last night she'd gone up to see him after Rick had dropped her off.

The young boy was hanging in there, but barely. So far, keeping his core body temperature down seemed to be helping to control his brain swelling. But she was afraid to hope. The repeat CT scan they'd done looked even worse than the first one.

His mother's face had been red and blotchy from crying. Not that she could blame the woman. Her husband had arrived, though, and even he'd been crying. Heck, every time she went to Tomas's bedside, she was tempted to cry, too.

The shrill sound of her phone startled her from her thoughts. She sat up, staring at the clock. Barely nine in the morning. The only place that normally called so early was the hospital.

She reached for the phone. "Hello?"

"Naomi Horton?"

She frowned at the strange voice. "Yes?"

"This is Amanda from the New Life Clinic. We've had a cancellation this morning and wondered if you wanted to reschedule your insemination appointment for today."

Reschedule for today? Speechless, her mind raced. The timing wasn't exactly perfect. The peak of her ovulation had been several days ago, but it was worth a try.

Faced with the possibility of actually getting pregnant, she wavered. Could she do this? Talking to Rick's sister, Jess, had reinforced what she'd originally thought, that being a single parent wasn't the worst thing in the world. Jess had as much admitted it, saying without hesitation that she'd do it all over again if given a choice.

Either she wanted a baby, or she didn't. And she'd researched the whole artificial insemination process at length. It wouldn't have been her first choice, but, then, having her husband leave her hadn't been her choice either.

Maybe the problem was with her, because deep down she knew that if things got serious, she'd have to tell the guy about her potential problems with fertility. She'd done that once with disastrous results.

Maybe Denis was just a jerk, but maybe not. Maybe lots of men would think less of her, the way Andrew and Denis both had.

"Yes," she said, before she could change her mind. "I'd love to come in."

"Good. If you could get here as soon as possible, that would be great."

As soon as possible. Naomi pulled on a pair of comfortable jeans and the nearest top she could find. There wasn't time to mess with her hair or to put on make-up. Besides, it wasn't as if she was going out on a date.

Although the result might be the same.

She swallowed a hysterical laugh as she strode out to the garage, climbed into her car and headed over to the New Life Clinic. Assailed by doubts, she picked up her cell phone twice to cancel, then put the phone down again, remembering her "Stay Alive, Just Drive" campaign. She'd had posters made and they were being plastered all over town.

She needed to set a good example, right?

Her stomach was clenched so hard it hurt by the time she pulled into the parking lot of the clinic. She sat in the car, debating the wisdom of what she was about to do, trying not to think about what Rick would say if he knew about her plan.

Not that his opinion mattered one way or the other. He'd made that much perfectly clear last night. She'd known a relationship was out of the question, but that fact didn't stop her from thinking about him.

Somehow she suspected Rick was a better man than either Andrew or Denis. She couldn't imagine him thinking less of her if he knew about her infertility.

Useless thoughts. Rick had lost his wife and daughter. He wasn't interested in her.

And she wanted a baby, not a man.

She flung open her car door and stepped out. Clutching her purse under her arm, she walked into the clinic. The atmosphere was nice, not your normal medical clinic environment. Amanda, the nice receptionist with very bright red hair, greeted her.

"I'm Naomi Horton, here to fill in a cancelled appointment?"

"Of course. We're so glad you could make it." Amanda handed over a clipboard of forms. "You'll just need to fill these out and we'll be ready to go."

"All right." Naomi did as she was told, her mouth dry, her stomach still hurting. Ignoring her inner doubts, she filled in the forms then handed over the clipboard.

"Come this way." Amanda led her to the exam room. "Take your clothes off just from the waist down and put this sheet over your lap. The doctor will be here in a few minutes."

"Thanks." Naomi felt funny, stripping down from just the waist only. She sat on the edge of the exam table, trying to tell herself this was no different than a routine pap smear. Nothing to be afraid of. A baby was worth a little discomfort.

"Hello, Naomi." Dr Curran greeted her with a broad smile and she noticed a female assistant following him into the room, just like during any other gynecological exam. Somewhere deep inside a rising bubble of hysteria almost made her leap off the exam table. "I'm so glad you could make it."

He walked her through the procedure, and she nodded her understanding even though her stomach felt worse with every second that passed. She tried not to panic as she lay back and allowed Dr Curran to begin the insemination process.

She stared at the ceiling, her chest so tight she could barely breathe. This wasn't the way she wanted her baby to be created. She wanted him or her to be conceived out of warmth. Out of love. Out of caring. What was she thinking, going this route? Maybe if she had a husband who was donating a part of himself, she'd feel differently. But she didn't.

She couldn't do it. "Stop."

Dr Curran paused and glanced at her in surprise. "Stop the procedure?"

"Yes." She clutched the sheet at her waist tightly. "I changed my mind. I can't do this."

He frowned. "Now, don't worry. Everyone gets a little nervous their first time. Maybe you just need a few minutes to relax?"

"No. I'm sorry." Relaxation techniques weren't going to help. Nothing was going to help. "I've really changed my mind. I don't want to get pregnant—at least, not like this."

"I see." Dr Curran exchanged a resigned look with his assistant, before stepping back and stripping off his gloves. "I'm afraid we don't do refunds."

She bit back a hysterical laugh. "I know. The money doesn't matter."

"You're welcome to come back if you change your mind again," he said with forced cheerfulness.

"Thanks," she said, as if she'd consider his suggestion, even though she knew she wouldn't. Naomi placed a hand over her abdomen, fighting a wave of nausea and wishing she'd taken the time to eat some breakfast.

Dr Curran and his assistant left her alone. She sat for several minutes, remembering all the appointments she'd cancelled over the past few months. Fate had been trying to tell her something. Obviously her subconscious knew what her brain had refused to admit. That this really wasn't what she wanted. In some tiny corner of her mind she'd known that while some women raved about this procedure, at least from what she had found in her research, it wasn't the right answer for her.

She would still love to have a family, but so far her success with relationships hasn't been stellar. Not just because of her erratic schedule, but because of her physical limitations to potentially getting pregnant. What man would want to enter into a relationship with her, not knowing if they'd ever have a family?

With a sigh she stepped down from the exam table and dressed again.

Maybe she needed to focus on the present and stop worrying about the unknown future. Her job was very stressful, it was possible Dr Curran was right. At least, about the part where she needed to relax. When was the last time she had done something just for fun? She couldn't remember, which meant she was well overdue.

And she couldn't help but think that Rick could also use a good dose of some lighthearted fun, too.

CHAPTER SEVEN

RICK stared down at Lizzy's peaceful, sleeping face, feeling as exhausted as if he'd gone ten rounds in a boxing ring. When Jess had called him at around one in the morning, telling him Lizzy was very sick, he'd immediately reacted to the panic in her tone.

Lizzy had gone to a birthday party on Saturday night, and the parents had served homemade pizza. Apparently there had been something wrong with the pork sausage, because Lizzy wasn't the only one who was sick. The only girls who hadn't gotten sick had been the ones who'd picked the sausage off their pizza, preferring to eat it plain.

Jess had called him when Lizzy had continued to throw up, long after her stomach had been empty. He'd taken one look at her pale, trembling and tear-stained face and brought her straight to the E.D. at Children's Memorial. The surgeon in him had assumed the worst, thinking there was something major wrong with her intestines, but in the end they'd diagnosed food poisoning.

After replacing many liters of IV fluids, the E.D.

physician had insisted on admitting her as a patient to make sure she didn't have a bad infection, like *E. coli* or something worse.

They'd gotten to Lizzy's room at about four in the morning. Jess had finally fallen asleep an hour later, when Lizzy had stopped throwing up. He hadn't been able to sleep, though, and felt as emotionally and physically drained as if he'd spent the whole night in the O.R. rather than watching over his sick niece.

For a while there he'd been very worried, more than he'd let on to Jess. Lizzy's small body had almost convulsed with the need to get whatever she had ingested out of her system. As a physician, he'd felt helpless to do anything much to ease her discomfort.

He scrubbed his hands over his face, noting that he needed to shave. And he should probably get something to eat. Would Naomi be in by now? Somewhere between five and six in the morning he'd wanted very badly to call her, despite his determination not to see her again on a personal level.

He didn't understand why he missed her so much. She'd only been a part of his life for less than a week, too short a time to become dependent on her.

The nurse peeked in to see how Lizzy was doing, but didn't wake her. He was really getting hungry, so he tiptoed out of Lizzy's room and headed down to the cafeteria. After getting something to eat, he made his way up to the PICU.

Memorizing the trauma call schedule had its advantages. He knew his own schedule, of course, but he also knew when everyone else was slotted to work. On the weekends they took twenty-four-hour call shifts to give other physicians more time off, and he knew Naomi was scheduled to start her twenty-four-hour shift at eight o'clock this morning.

As he strode down the hall towards Tomas's room, he realized he hadn't thought of Gabrielle or Sarah in a few days. Since he'd kissed Naomi. The flash of guilt slowed his pace until he stood just outside Tomas's door, seeing Naomi seated in a chair beside his bed.

There was no sign of Tomas's parents and he suspected Naomi had insisted they get something to eat. His gaze automatically went to the boy's bedside monitor, and he winced when he saw Tomas's ICP reading in the high thirties.

Naomi was lightly stroking the boy's head, smoothing his blond hair away from his face. Most of his body was covered with a cooling blanket as part of the hypothermia protocol. When he saw the sheen of tears in her eyes, he quickly took a step back, uncomfortable with displays of emotion.

Too late. She lifted her head and saw him standing there. She sniffed and brushed away the evidence of her tears as she stood.

He tucked his hands in the pockets of his jeans. He shouldn't really be in the ICU dressed so casually, but he wasn't officially on duty either. He lifted his chin towards the monitor. "His ICP is worse."

"Yes." She shook her head, her expression grim. "I'm afraid it's only a matter of time. The hypothermia protocol has slowed down the swelling, but not enough. We've done everything, even removed a portion of his cranium, but I'm afraid the damage to his brain is too severe."

"Where are his parents?" he asked.

"Getting some breakfast. They should be back any minute." Naomi dropped her gaze as if embarrassed. "I told them I'd stay with Tomas while they were gone."

It was on the tip of his tongue to remind her not to get too personally involved with her patients when Tomas's parents returned.

"Thanks for staying with him," his mother said.

"You're welcome." Naomi's smile was sad. "You both deserved to eat at least one meal together. You've been taking turns since Tomas was admitted." She stepped back to give Tomas's parents room to sit beside his bed.

Naomi caught up to Rick when he started to leave. "Rick? What happened? You look awful." Her eyes widened and she grabbed his arm. "Frank?"

"No, Frank is fine," he hastened to reassure her. "I spoke to Hilda, his wife, and she said he didn't need surgery, the stent in his coronary artery seems to be doing the trick." He turned to Naomi. "We'll still have to cover his shifts for a while, though. He's off work for at least three weeks."

"I understand." She didn't argue, but was still giving him an odd look. "Chuck was on call last night, so why do you look worse than he did?"

"Lizzy's been sick." By unspoken agreement they drifted into the physicians' conference room. As it was Sunday, the residents weren't camped out in there the way they usually were. Residents didn't need to come in over the weekends unless they were on call, too. "So, yeah, I've been up most of the night."

"Lizzy's sick?" Naomi's voice rose in alarm. She gripped his forearm. "What happened?"

"Food poisoning is the working diagnosis," he told her. "She's up on the fifth floor as an inpatient. She was at a birthday party yesterday where the parents served homemade pizza and we think there was something wrong with the pork sausage. The kids who didn't get sick didn't eat any of the sausage."

"Oh, no. I'm sorry." Naomi's voice held genuine concern. One of the things he liked most about Naomi was that she cared. She truly cared about people. Tomas, Lizzy, Emily, Tristan.

Him.

"Jess was pretty stressed out. Lizzy was so sick we were really worried something far worse was wrong with her." He scowled, thinking of the useless guy who'd made his sister pregnant and then disappeared off the face of the earth. Obviously, he didn't care. "I'm glad it was nothing worse than food poisoning. Being a surgeon, I immediately thought the worst, necrotic bowel or something equally deadly."

"I'd like to go up and see her. Do you think Jess would mind?" she asked, letting her hand fall away. He resisted the urge to reach for her.

"Of course she wouldn't mind." He rubbed his hand over his stubbly cheek, wishing he'd brought a razor. Naomi probably thought he looked like a bum. "When I left, they were both sleeping, but I'm sure they'll be awake by now."

He walked with her through the PICU, down the

hall and to the elevator. "Frank is scheduled to work on Tuesday night. I'll take his call shift."

Naomi nodded. "I'm on duty for days on Tuesday, so if you want me to stay later, let me know."

If he hadn't known better, he'd think some divine intervention was making their shifts overlap on purpose. Not that he thought Frank had planned on having a heart attack. "I should be fine."

She fell silent as they walked down the hall towards Lizzy's room. When they got closer, he could hear the sound of the television.

"Hi, Uncle Rick," Lizzy said with a weak smile.

"I wondered where you'd disappeared to." Jess sat up on her cot, yawning widely.

"I brought you a visitor." He stepped aside so they could see Naomi. He leaned over to give Lizzy a kiss. "We've all been worried about you, kiddo."

"How are you feeling, Lizzy?" Naomi asked.

"My stomach still hurts." Lizzy gently rubbed her tummy. "I think the muscles are sore."

"I wouldn't be surprised," Naomi agreed. She glanced over at Rick's sister. "Hi, Jess. Is there anything you need?"

"No, we're fine." Jess waved a hand toward her daughter. "Especially now that Lizzy is feeling better." Jess sighed. "It was a worrying night, though."

"I bet." Naomi's gaze was sympathetic.

He watched as Naomi chatted with Jess and Lizzy, struck by how she already seemed to be part of the family.

Her pager beeped. She unclipped it from her trousers and read the text message. The color drained from her face, and her worried gaze caught his. "Tomas. I have to go."

"I understand." He wanted very badly to go with her, but he wasn't on call or on duty.

"I'll try to stop by to check on you both later," Naomi said, stepping towards the door. "Take care."

He followed her out the door, watching as she quickened her pace, rushing down the hall. He didn't doubt that something had happened to Tomas.

And he couldn't help but suspect the worst.

Naomi rushed into Tomas's room, her heart dropping when she saw that his ICP was zero.

Dear God, his brain swelling had cut off his blood flow. She rounded on the resident in the room. "What happened?"

The resident, Dr McKay, looked scared to death. "His ICP went to sixty and his blood pressure was sky high, too. Suddenly it shot down to nothing."

Damn. *Damn.* "Get a CT of his head stat," she ordered, knowing it was probably already too late.

"We lost all reflexes," Doreen said in a low voice. "He didn't have a lot before, but now everything is gone."

If the nurse was right, there was no point in doing another CT scan. Her shoulders slumped with the reality of what had happened. "Wait. Hold off on the CT scan." She did her own neuro examination, realizing Doreen was right. His reflexes were gone. Clinically, Tomas was brain dead. She swallowed hard. "Get a brain-flow study instead."

Doreen nodded. "I'll call Radiology."

"I'll talk to his parents." Naomi didn't look forward to that discussion at all. At times like this, she just didn't know what to say. With all the modern technology in medicine, why did such a young boy have to die? She didn't have any answers.

She found Tomas's parents in the waiting room. The moment they saw her serious face, Tomas's mother burst into tears.

"He's gone," Tomas's father said in a flat tone. "You're coming to tell us he's gone."

"I'm afraid so." Naomi didn't want to give them any false hope. "It looks as if he doesn't have any blood flow to his brain but I'm going to get a brain-flow study to make sure."

Tomas's mother lifted her tear-streaked face from her husband's shoulder. "If he is gone, I want to donate his organs."

"Jeannie—" her husband began, but she cut him off.

"I want to donate his organs," Tomas's mother repeated firmly. "I want something good to come of this."

The generosity of people never ceased to amaze Naomi. She swallowed against the lump in her throat and nodded. "I'll see what we can do. First we need to get the results of his brain-flow study. Then we'll go from there."

The process wasn't quick or easy. Naomi called the organ procurement organization and they came to assess Tomas. He was a promising candidate. The results of his first brain-flow study was negative, showing no brain flow, but they needed to wait another six hours and repeat the clinical exam again, just to make sure.

Angie found her a couple of hours later. "Naomi? Is it true Tomas is going to be a donor?"

She nodded. "Yes, his parents have already given their permission. Why?"

Angie twisted her fingers nervously. "Tomas has the same blood type as Emily Brown, and they're about the same size. It's possible she'll get his heart."

Good grief, she hadn't thought of that. But what Angie had said was absolutely right. Pediatric donors were hard to find because not only did you have to get the same blood type matched, but size became an important factor, too. You couldn't put a two-year-old's heart into a ten-year-old, or vice versa.

"Have you heard from the organ procurement people on this?" she asked, hoping Angie was right. "Don't say anything to Emily or to Tristan until we're sure. Emily might not be the highest recipient on the donor list."

"They just called me," Angie admitted. "I was told to get Emily worked up for possible surgery. If his heart is good, they're planning to give Emily the transplant."

As happy as Naomi was for Emily, she still grieved for Tomas. And for his family.

Six hours later, Tomas was pronounced dead. Naomi insisted on giving the family all the time they needed to say goodbye.

She went into Emily's room, where the little girl was awake and sitting up in bed, still connected to the ventilator, holding her brother's hand.

"Hi, Emily. Hi, Tristan." She couldn't believe how well they were both doing, even though Tristan's leg was still in traction.

"Hi, Doc," Tristan greeted her, as Emily couldn't talk with the breathing tube in. "Is it true? Is Em getting a heart?"

"Yes, it's true." Naomi tried to smile.

"Because someone died?" Tristan persisted.

"Yes." She could feel her throat getting choked up and fought to keep her voice steady. "But also because some very kind parents wanted to give the gift of life. Emily is the lucky child who will receive the gift."

Tristan clutched Emily's hand. "When will she go to surgery?"

"Soon." Naomi smiled at Emily, who was listening to their conversation with wide eyes. "I know you're probably scared, Emily, but you'll be so much happier off that machine. Just think, in a few more days you'll probably be well enough to get out of the ICU." Barring any complications, that was.

Emily nodded, indicating she understood.

Naomi left the room, searching for Angie. "Have the nurses arranged for Emily's mother to visit lately?"

"Not in a couple of days. She was here once, after she'd been taken off the ventilator, but then we heard she took a turn for the worse and ended up getting re-intubated," Angie explained. "Their dad is doing better, though. He's awake and following commands. He should get off the ventilator and get transferred out of the ICU soon. The transplant team went over to Trinity to get a signed consent for the surgery from the father."

"Good." She glanced up to see the OR transplant

team coming to fetch Emily. Standing out of their way, she watched as they connected Emily to all the portable monitoring equipment and then wheeled her away.

Naomi couldn't shake her overwhelming sadness, though. It just wasn't fair that one child had to die so another child could live.

Naomi didn't see much of Rick over the next week as he was busy with the level-one re-verification process. Apparently the site visit went very well, because after the survey was over, everyone was smiling.

She missed talking to Rick. The only time she saw him was at work, and their conversations were pretty much limited to patient care issues. She did find out that Lizzy had been discharged home and was already back at school, without any lingering affects from her food-poisoning episode.

Emily was doing great after her heart transplant. It was almost as if Tomas's heart had been meant for her. She did better than any other transplant recipient that Naomi had ever seen. She wasn't the primary physician any more, the CT surgery team had taken over her care, but she still checked on Emily every chance she got. After a few days in the ICU, Emily had been taken off the breathing machine and could talk. The first word she spoke was her brother's name. Tristan.

By the end of the second week, Naomi was feeling exhausted. Between them, they'd covered all of Frank's shifts to the point she felt as if she lived at the hospital.

No wonder she didn't have a personal life to speak of.

No wonder Andrew had been planning to leave her.

She shook off the depressing thought. What she needed to do was to spend her next few days off, relaxing and having fun. Steve and Dirk were back from San Francisco, and they'd picked up several of Frank's shifts. Now that she'd given up her dream of having a baby on her own, it was time she considered what she wanted out of her life.

"Naomi?" Rick called her name as she was walking toward the door, having just reported off to Steve.

"Yes?" She turned to watch him catch up to her. He looked great, relaxed for the first time in days, and she had to stop herself from asking what his plans were for the weekend.

Professional. Their relationship was purely professional.

And maybe if she told herself that several times a day, she'd start to believe it.

"Dirk told me you're presenting at the Society of Critical Care Medicine conference in Chicago next weekend."

She raised a curious brow. "Yes, that's right." Then she realized why he was asking. "I forgot, Frank was supposed to present with me."

"Exactly." Rick grinned. "I didn't realize you were part of the presentation too, but I told Frank I'd cover his portion. He's at home, recuperating well, and I stopped over there last night so he could give me his presentation."

Instead of feeling bad for Frank, her heart gave a betraying leap of excitement. "Really? That's great."

His expression turned serious for a moment. "I hope you don't mind doing the presentation with me."

"Of course not." Okay, so maybe spending a weekend alone with Rick in Chicago might be a little awkward, but she was pretty sure she could control herself. Maybe. Definitely. "I planned on taking the train down on Friday morning—we're part of the opening panel of presenters on Friday evening."

"Sounds good. I'll ride down with you."

"Great. We can compare notes on the train."

He took a step towards the door. "I guess I should let you go. Do you have plans for the weekend?"

Her heart thudded again. "No plans. How about you?"

"Lizzy has a volleyball picnic on Sunday that I need to go to." His eyes brightened. "Would you like to come with me?"

She hid a flash of disappointment. Not that she didn't like spending time with Jess and Lizzy, but clearly, he didn't want to see her alone. She understood why. After all, she knew as well as he did that their relationship was strictly professional.

She should refuse. But she didn't have anything better to do, and the thought of the long, lonely weekend stretching before her made her nod in agreement. "Sure, I'd love to come."

"Lizzy will be thrilled," Rick said. "I'll call you to let you know the times."

She watched him walk away, wishing she could prise him out of her mind. Rick wasn't good for her, she knew that. Hadn't he told her he couldn't offer a future?

And she'd informed him she didn't do flings. So

where did that leave them? Nowhere. Absolutely nowhere.

Except maybe to share a little bit of fun and companionship.

She tried to tell herself that a friendly relationship with Rick would be enough, but wasn't so sure she believed it.

CHAPTER EIGHT

RICK didn't know what had possessed him to invite Naomi to Lizzy's volleyball picnic, but when she showed up at Rainbow Park wearing a pair of tiny red shorts and a white halter top, a stab of lust hit deep, robbing his brain of rational thought.

Obviously his physical desire was part of the reason he'd invited her, but in that case, his rash decision hadn't been too smart. Spending time with the woman who haunted his dreams was not the way to keep his distance.

He wanted her. Badly. And he didn't know what to do about it.

"Hi, Rick." Naomi's greeting was cheerful and friendly, and she turned to include his sister and Lizzy. "Jess, Lizzy. How are you?"

"Great, Naomi." Jess grinned. "Glad you could make it. Do you play volleyball?"

Naomi laughed. "You realize I'm too short to be a good volleyball player, don't you? But I'll play. I can fake it with the best of them."

"I don't care if you're short, I want you on my team," Lizzy declared loyally. "You, too, Uncle Rick."

"Sounds good." He glanced at Naomi, trying not to notice how she looked like a candy cane, only twice as good. "You don't have to play if you don't want to."

She gave a slight shrug. "I don't mind. Just don't expect me to spike the ball when playing the front line. I'll be lucky if I can reach the net.

He thought she was perfect the way she was. "Would you like something to drink?"

"Water would be great."

He nodded and walked over to the makeshift food stand. He paid for two bottles of water, the proceeds going to support the girls' volleyball team. On his way back, he saw Naomi laughing at something Lizzy was saying and his body tightened with awareness.

Damn. He was in trouble. Deep, deep trouble. While a part of him he was secretly glad to know his sex drive wasn't dead, he resented the way his body didn't listen to the cool logic of his brain.

Naomi wasn't for him. She wanted more than a simple, no-strings physical relationship. Just the thought of entering anything more complicated cooled his body's response.

He walked over and handed her the bottle of water. She thanked him and then tipped her head back to take a drink. He caught himself momentarily mesmerized by her neck, then lower still to the shadowed cleavage in the V of her halter top.

Swallowing hard, he resisted the urge to dump his bottle of cold water over his head. He took a step back, grimly acknowledging that it would be a miracle if he made it through the day without touching her.

"Come on, everyone, it's time to play!" Lizzy

jumped up from the picnic table and dashed over to where several volleyball courts were set up. Teams were already being assembled.

Rick, Naomi and Jess followed Lizzy over to the grass-covered volleyball courts. The participants were split up into teams of six, and their foursome was paired with a guy by the name of Jeff and his daughter Amber.

The adults quickly introduced themselves, Rick vaguely remembered having seen Jeff and Amber on the night of the father-daughter dance. He was wondering where Amber's mother was when Jeff flashed Naomi an admiring glance.

The ball sailed over the net, nearly hitting Rick in the head, bringing his attention back to the game. In the beginning, the game was lighthearted and fun, but when the score was tied and the game-winning point was on the line, things quickly turned tense.

They waited breathlessly for the serve. The ball shot over the net in a fast line drive.

"I got it!" Jeff shouted, leaping up to hit at the ball. Just at the same moment Naomi moved to do the same. She pulled back, but not quickly enough. Jeff hit the ball, sending it sailing over the net, but on the way down smacked her in the head with his elbow, hard enough to cause a loud cracking sound.

Naomi gave a low cry and crumpled to the ground. For a split second there was a stunned silence. Rick moved first, then everyone rushed over.

"Naomi? Are you okay?" Jeff's expression was twisted with guilt.

Rick dropped to his knees on the other side of her,

his heart pounding in his chest when he realized she hadn't moved. "Naomi?" His breath caught in his throat and he quickly checked for a pulse, feeling only slightly relieved when he found the thready beat. She was breathing, but the blow to her head had knocked her out cold. "Someone get me an ice pack," he shouted.

"Here," one of the volleyball coaches, ever prepared, handed him a cold pack.

His hands shook with a fine tremor as he placed the cold pack over her pale forehead. Naomi grimaced and her eyelids fluttered open, her gaze momentarily unfocused. "Ouch. My head hurts."

She was all right. Relieved, he subtly checked her pupils to make sure she didn't have a concussion or worse, his heart slowly resuming its normal rhythm in his chest.

"I'm so sorry," Jeff apologized, looking miserable. "I can't believe I hurt you."

"It's all right." Naomi reached up to the ice pack, her fingertips brushing his hand. "My fault. I'm not very athletic I'm afraid."

"Don't get up yet," Rick cautioned when she moved as if to sit up. "Just give yourself a few minutes first. Lizzy?" He glanced at his niece, who was staring down at Naomi with faint alarm. "Will you get Naomi another bottle of water?"

"Sure." Lizzy seemed happy to have something to do and hurried off.

"I'm such a dope." Jeff was still berating himself. "I don't know what's wrong with me. This was supposed to be a nice, friendly game, not a competitive one."

"Don't worry about it." She smiled, and Rick had to restrain himself from interrupting when she reached for Jeff's hand. "Did we win?"

Jeff let out a wry laugh. "We did. The ball hit the ground on their side because everyone was worried about you."

"Good. My ruse worked." She winced again, but then turned her attention to Rick. "Help me up. I feel foolish, lying here like this."

Lizzy came back with the bottle of water, and Naomi sat up and took a sip. She grimaced a little, but didn't give any other sign of being injured. After a few minutes she gingerly rose to her feet. Rick was a little irritated at the way Jeff continued to stick around. Didn't the guy have a wife somewhere?

Naomi kept the ice pack pressed to her head as they made their way over to their picnic table.

"Do you have a headache?" he asked with a frown. "I could try to scrounge up some aspirin."

"A little," she admitted, sitting down gingerly. "I'll be fine."

He wasn't so sure. Her face was pale and she moved slowly as if sudden movements sent excruciating pain through her head. Where was that first-aid kit? There had to be some aspirin in there.

The kit was near the volleyball court, so he went over to search for the medication. He headed back to the table, his steps slowing to a stop, a thrust of jealousy hitting him hard when he saw Jeff sitting right beside Naomi.

"Better watch out, I think he's trying to move in on your date," Jess murmured from beside him.

"She's not my date," he automatically corrected her, trying to ignore his resentment. He flashed the guy a dark look. "Isn't he married?"

"Divorced." The fleeting wistfulness in Jess's eyes squeezed his heart. "He's the hot catch around here. Most of the single moms have their eye on him."

Including his sister, Rick guessed. Dammit, he didn't know anything about the guy, but he already didn't like him. Rick didn't say anything more, but crossed over to give Naomi her aspirin.

The rest of the picnic passed uneventfully. Jeff and Amber finally left, going back to their own picnic table and leaving them alone. But Rick noticed there was a small white business card in Naomi's hand, and when he narrowed his gaze on the tiny print he saw Jeff's name and number.

When she tucked the card into her purse, he had to bury a flash of anger. Naomi had a right to see whomever she wanted. He didn't have any claim on her.

But as they left the park, walking back to their cars, he couldn't deny a deep surge of possessiveness. He didn't want Naomi to call Jeff.

Not now. Not ever.

Naomi didn't see Rick on Monday, but that evening when she arrived home, he called her.

"How are you feeling?" he asked.

Him contacting her at home seemed oddly intimate, although she knew he might just be checking up on her because he was the boss and cared about the members of his staff. "I'm fine."

"No headache?" he persisted.

"Maybe a small one," she allowed. "But nothing worth getting worried about. I'm sure it will be gone by tomorrow."

"Do you need me to find someone else to staff the PICU tomorrow?" he asked. "In case your headache isn't gone by then?"

"No, I'll be fine." She strove for a light tone. "But I was thinking of asking you to cover my Fourth of July call shift as payback for covering your father-daughter dance. What do you think?"

"No problem." She'd been teasing but he responded with total seriousness. "I told you I owed you a favor and I meant it."

"Sold," she said with a laugh. She didn't actually have plans, but hoped to have a personal life someday. "Fourth of July is always nuts," she warned. "Don't plan on getting much sleep."

He groaned. "I won't." A pause, then, "I'll let you go. I just wanted to check on you to make sure there were no lingering effects from your head injury."

She made an exasperated sound. "Don't be so dramatic. I didn't have a head injury."

"Maybe not, but I was the one looking down at you while you were out cold."

She didn't know what to say to that. She willed her racing heart to slow down. "Good night, Rick. See you tomorrow."

"Good night, Naomi." The husky note in his voice when he said her name made her knees tremble.

She hung up and turned toward the kitchen table, where she'd left Jeff's business card. Jeff was a much better choice than Rick. A safe bet for sure. First, because he was a really nice guy, he'd felt awful about accidentally hitting her in the head with his elbow. Second, he already had a daughter, Amber, so he might not care if she couldn't have any more children. He also ran his own carpentry business, so maybe he wouldn't mind her chaotic hours.

So if he was perfect, why hadn't she called him?

With a sigh she spun away. No matter how she told herself Jeff was the logical choice, she couldn't get her mind off Rick.

Her boss. Her brain knew Rick Weber was the wrong man for her but her body—no, actually her heart—didn't care. Rick cared about people, even if he tried to bury his emotions where they didn't show. Remembering the way he'd stayed up all night with Lizzy when she was sick warmed her heart. And just now, the moment she'd recognized his voice on the phone, her pulse had quickened with excitement, betraying her true feelings.

Yesterday, when she'd been knocked unconscious, Rick had been so attentive, so caring. And when Jeff had taken a seat beside her, while Rick had hunted down the first-aid kit for aspirin, she'd caught the flash of annoyance in Rick's eyes. Had he been momentarily jealous? The essentially female part of her hoped so.

Yet even if Rick was starting to care about her, there was still the issue of him being her boss. Did they ever make exceptions to the no-relationship rule? She hoped so.

She wanted to believe that if work hadn't been in the way, Rick would allow whatever it was that simmered between them a chance to blossom, to grow into something more. He'd claimed not to have anything to offer, but she didn't really believe him.

He was clearly wounded by his past, but he had plenty to offer. His concern over her proved that. He had enough to offer that she couldn't even consider trying to find someone else to go out with.

With a determined gesture she picked up Jeff's business card and tossed it in the garbage.

She'd see Rick again tomorrow as he was on trauma call on days, and it was her turn to staff the PICU during the same shift.

She couldn't wait.

The day was slow, no major crises until four-fifteen in the afternoon, when her pager went off for a ten-year-old girl with multiple gunshot wounds, an innocent victim of a violent fight outside a downtown shopping mall. Even though it was her job to work in the PICU, things were under control, so she headed down to the O.R. to see if she could help.

By the time she got there and changed into scrubs, Rick already had the patient in the O.R. She'd checked briefly on the girl's parents, who were beside themselves, before finding him. He barely looked up at her when she walked in.

"Need help?" she asked from behind her surgical mask.

His eyes met hers. "It's bad. There's a lot of damage."

He hadn't actually asked for help, but he hadn't

told her to get lost either. She kicked her step stool over to the opposite side of the girl and began to assist.

Rick was right, the poor girl was a mess. Way worse than Emily's case, and that had been the hardest in her entire career.

"How many bullets did she take?" she asked, horrified by the volume of blood that was being sucked out of the way. She grabbed a suture and began tying off bleeders.

"Three. One in the pelvis lodged in her kidney, the other two did a lot of damage to her stomach, liver and intestines." Rick's voice was devoid of emotion, but his eyes were dark with worry when he met her gaze. "She's bleeding from everywhere."

"Is her aorta hit?" She couldn't see how the largest artery in the body could have been missed, considering how bullets often ricocheted once inside the abdomen.

"Not that I can tell." His voice was grim. "With so many bleeding vessels it's hard to see."

"Blood pressure dropping, eighty over thirty-six." The anesthesiologist gave them the bad news. "I have her on two different vasopressors, and so far they're not working."

"How much blood have you given?" Rick asked.

"Ten units."

For a child of her size that was a lot of blood. "I'll tie off bleeders while you explore." She took over for him, doing her best to get the girl's bleeding under control.

He swore. "Her descending aorta was hit and I

found a bullet lodged in her diaphragm. There's still one bullet unaccounted for."

Her stomach twisted, understanding his concern. If the diaphragm was injured, the girl would probably spend the rest of her life on a ventilator. Without the movement of a diaphragm, a person's lungs didn't work.

"How bad is the aorta?" The largest bleeding vessel had to be their first concern. "Can you fix it?"

"Blood pressure down to sixty," the anesthesiologist said in a loud voice. "Just gave two more units of blood. We're losing her."

"I'm trying." Sweat dampened his forehead and one of the nurses blotted away the worst of it. Rick acted as if he didn't even notice. "Dammit, she's already got some lower vessel ischemia."

When there wasn't enough blood and oxygen getting to the tissues and organs, the tissue died, causing ischemia. Desperately, she kept finding and tying off bleeding vessels with the intention of going back and reconnecting the arteries and veins, but she could tell they were fighting a losing battle.

"Blood pressure forty-eight systolic. No pulse."

"No!" Rick abandoned what he was doing and began performing chest compressions. "Dammit, she can't die. She can't!"

Naomi saw the extent of the tissue necrosis in the girl's abdomen and knew it was already too late. Even if they could get her heart back, her intestines and most of her liver were already dead from lack of blood flow.

"Rick, don't." She put a hand over his, trying to stop his chest compressions. "It's too late. She's gone."

He stopped, closed his eyes, and stood with his hands still in the center of the girl's chest. Everybody else stopped what they were doing too.

Naomi swallowed hard and glanced at the O.R. nurses, who were watching Rick with unveiled sympathy. "Time of death, five-ten p.m. She'll need an autopsy so take care with the body."

Rick stepped back then, stripping off his bloody gloves and throwing them into a nearby garbage can before he stalked out of the O.R. suite.

She took a few moments to make sure the death notice was signed before trying to go after him. She ripped off her bloody clothes, washed her hands in the scrub sinks outside the door, and then went to find Rick.

She found him in the O.R. physicians' lounge. He'd cleaned up a little, but still had his face mask dangling from his neck and his O.R. hat on as he sat with his head cradled in his hands.

"Hey." She cautiously approached. "Are you all right?"

Stupid question, because she could see for herself he wasn't all right.

"She was ten, the same age as Lizzy," he murmured, without looking up. "And now she's dead."

"Rick, you did your best. You didn't give up. You kept going when most physicians would have stopped."

He sighed and lifted his head. "I kept thinking of Lizzy, kept thinking of the poor parents who were going to miss their daughter. I couldn't stop, because I couldn't find my usual detachment."

Detachment? The phrase bothered her. "Maybe that's okay. Maybe you're a better surgeon without the protection of your detachment."

His anguished gaze met hers. "Then why is she dead? *Why?*"

She sensed he was asking about his own daughter more than the young girl he'd just operated on. The intensity of his pain tore at her. "Because you know as well as I do that we can't save everyone. We don't decide who lives and who dies. I'm sorry about Sarah." Her voice wavered. "I know how much you loved your daughter."

CHAPTER NINE

SARAH. Sweet little Sarah. The pressure in his chest increased and he suddenly needed to leave. To get away. "I have to go." Abruptly Rick stood and strode toward the door. If he stayed here with Naomi for a minute longer, he'd lose it. Her gentle empathy was too much to bear.

"Wait." She snagged his arm. He stopped and stared at her small hand for a moment. "Are you going to the family center? Do you want me to come along?"

Family center? He sucked in a harsh breath. Of course. How could he have forgotten? Someone had to go down and talk to Mary's parents.

It was his duty as the surgeon of record to explain what had happened.

"No, I'll be fine." He didn't feel fine at all, but he stoically held onto the thin thread of control. "You need to meet Dirk up in the PICU to make rounds."

She hesitated and he could tell she wanted to argue, but she finally nodded. "All right. Are you going straight home afterwards?"

The idea of going home didn't appeal in the least.

"I don't know. I should get some dinner. We could both get some." The offer popped out of his mouth before he realized what he was saying.

"I'd like that." She flashed him a gentle smile. "See you upstairs."

He nodded and followed her out of the O.R. lounge. He gathered himself, searching for the inner strength he'd need to face a young girl's grieving parents.

The courage he'd need to tell them their daughter was dead.

Feeling emotionally drained after talking to Mary's parents, he headed back up to the PICU to meet Naomi. He was half-tempted to cancel their plans. After everything he'd been through, he wouldn't be very good company.

But when she turned and smiled at him, he didn't say a word. As much as he felt battered, he really didn't want to be alone either.

"Are you ready to go?" she asked.

"Yeah." He feared his emotional detachment was back. His face felt frozen and Naomi's expression turned from welcoming to troubled. He almost felt as if it were someone else making dinner plans as he suggested they pick up Chinese and take it back to his house.

"Sounds good." Her gaze searched his questioningly. "I'll follow you."

She paused at her car, which he was disconcerted to realize was parked right next to his. He tried to smile, but didn't think he was too successful. He quickly called in a take-out order and fifteen minutes later their food was ready.

His condo complex was just down the street. He pulled into the garage so there was room for Naomi to park in the driveway.

Carrying the bag holding their dinners, he unlocked the door and held it open for her. Flipping on lights as he went, he headed into the kitchen.

"Make yourself at home," he offered. "Something to drink?" He opened the cupboard and reached for two glasses.

"Just water, thanks." Naomi didn't sit at the table, but stood and glanced around. His kitchen and living room were really one big open room. "Nice place. Although your walls are a little bare."

"Yeah, I know." He grimaced. "Jess has been telling me the same thing."

"Do you have any pictures? Of Gabrielle and Sarah?"

He froze. His fingers tightened around the glasses so hard he feared the glass would shatter in his hands. He forced himself to relax. "In a photo album somewhere."

The troubled expression was back in her eyes. "I'd like to see them."

For a moment his vision blurred and he carefully set the glasses on the table, before he dropped them. "Maybe later."

"Rick." Naomi crossed over to him. "Why are you doing this?"

"What?" Warning bells jangled in his brain. It had been a mistake, inviting her here when he was internally such a mess from losing Mary. He didn't want to talk about his past. His family.

"Shutting them out of your life." She put a hand on his arm. "Refusing to give in to your grief. This is the second time you've come close to revealing how you really feel, then suddenly you're gone."

He stared at her, fighting his emotions.

"I saw the look on your face after you lost Mary," she continued. "But now you're acting like some robot instead of a man who knows exactly what it's like to lose a daughter."

He wanted to deny what she was saying, but couldn't. Because she was right. He felt exactly like a robot. The pressure in his chest was back and he struggled to breathe.

Gabrielle. And Sarah. His baby. His daughter. Sarah was gone. And like the child he had just lost, she wasn't ever coming back.

"Rick?" Naomi came close, wrapped her arms around him. He stiffened, searching for the strength to break free. He didn't want to lose it, not here. Not now. He told himself to back off, to put some distance between them, but his muscles didn't listen to his command. Instead, his arms hauled Naomi close, and he lowered his head, burying his face in her hair. "It's okay to show your feelings for Gabrielle and Sarah. I know how much you cared about them," she whispered.

Tears he'd never shed in the two years since Sarah's death burned the back of his throat and pierced his eyeballs, threatening to gush forth like a geyser of sorrow and angst. Somehow, through the funeral and for days afterwards, when he'd packed up all of Gabrielle's and Sarah's things, he never broke down. Never felt as if he was going to fly apart in grief. He'd walled off all emotion, and had insisted on returning to work, anxious to do something that would help him maintain the barrier of emotional distance. Focusing on work had meant he didn't need to face his loss.

He'd held back the helplessness for two full years.

Yet suddenly he couldn't deny his grief any longer.

He took several ragged, deep breaths as the sorrow dug deep. Inside, he railed at the unfairness of losing his little girl. She'd been so young. Too young to die.

Memories danced through his mind. Sarah's birth. Her first smile. When she'd learned to roll over and to crawl. Throwing her food on the floor from her highchair in a temper tantrum. Resting her tiny head on his shoulder when she'd been tired. Learning to walk.

So many firsts. Yet not nearly enough.

Eventually the sharp angst faded, easing the tightness of his chest. He was surprised to discover Naomi's hair felt damp beneath his cheek. He should have been embarrassed, but there wasn't room inside him to care.

He didn't know how long they stood together, locked in a tight embrace. Minutes could have been hours for all he knew.

At some point the havoc and pain inside him subtly changed to something different. Comfort. Acceptance. Peace. And with the softer emotions came tingling physical awareness.

Naomi. Her soft curves cushioning his hardness. The subtle pine scent that clung to her hair and skin.

The gentleness of her touch as she stroked his shoulders and back.

Her touch became sensual, or at least it was now that he was aware of it. She was such a caring woman, he never wanted to let her go. His groin tightened with need, and he had to stop himself from pulling her even tighter against him. She must have felt the change within him because she lifted her head and pushed her tangled, damp hair away from her face. Her eyes searched his. "Rick?"

His name on her lips sent a harpoon of longing deep into his soul. She was so beautiful, his chest ached. He wanted to kiss her. He longed to lose himself in her, to know every inch of her body as well as he knew his own.

Unable to resist, he lowered his mouth to hers.

Her lips softened, parted and he groaned and deepened the kiss, the way he'd wanted since the first time he'd held her in his arms.

He wanted her. Needed this, after being alone for so long. He kissed her as if his life depended on her sustenance.

With an abrupt move she pulled away, placing a hand on the center of his chest. "Wait."

He stared at her, breath sawing in and out of his lungs. He scrambled to make his brain cells work. "What's wrong?"

"I…think we'd better stop."

He realized her scrub top had become untucked from her drawstring pants. Had he done that? He took a step back. "I'm sorry."

"Rick, you don't have to be sorry." Naomi's tone

held a note of exasperation. "It's just…" She hesitated, and then continued, "I don't want you to confuse your feelings for Gabrielle with your feelings for me."

"Naomi, I care about you." He sighed, realizing he'd made a mess of things. Again. "Trust me, I wasn't thinking of Gabrielle just now, I was only thinking of you."

Her brow furrowed. "I wish I could believe that."

He obviously owed her an explanation. "Let's eat," he suggested. "I'll tell you a little about my relationship with my wife."

Naomi nodded, and tightened her drawstring pants as she walked to the kitchen table. "Smells good."

"We can warm the containers in the microwave if the food is too cold." He opened the closest container, grateful to discover the food was still lukewarm. "What do you think? Should we heat them up?"

"No, it's fine." She sat across from him and took the fork he handed her from the silverware drawer. "Thanks."

He took a bite of his egg roll and tried to think about where to begin. "Gabrielle and I were married for just two years before we had Sarah. She never liked my erratic schedule, but after Sarah was born things seemed to get better, at least for a while."

A shadow darkened her eyes. "Yes, I know what you mean. A trauma surgeon's schedule isn't easy to put up with."

She spoke as if she knew only too well what he and Gabrielle had gone through. "It wasn't just the long hours. The bigger issue for Gabrielle was simply being alone. She came from a large family, always had lots of people around. In fact, she shared an apartment with two of her sisters before we were married." He stared at his food for a moment. "She used to call me all the time because she wanted someone to talk to. But often I was in the middle of surgery or in a complicated trauma resuscitation and couldn't talk."

"What happened?"

"She told me she was thinking of leaving me. That she didn't think she was cut out to be the wife of a surgeon."

"I'm sorry," Naomi murmured.

"I asked if she'd be willing to try and work things out, but she claimed she needed some time and space to think about it. I'd like to believe I could have changed her mind, but the night she was moving home to live with her parents was the night she and Sarah crashed."

The night they had both died.

"How awful for you."

He didn't want to talk about this, but felt he owed it to Naomi to be honest. "For the longest time I couldn't grieve, couldn't let go of my emotions—until tonight." He forced himself to meet her gaze. He should have felt embarrassed for losing it in front of Naomi, but she gave him a sense of peace. "I felt so guilty over being a lousy husband and father. As if I deserved to lose them."

"No, Rick." Naomi reached over to touch his arm. "You didn't deserve to lose them, just like Mary's parents didn't deserve to lose their daughter." She lifted her shoulders in a helpless shrug. "There aren't any easy answers as to why some people lose the ones they love."

"I guess not." He pushed his half-eaten Chinese food away. "But I need you to know, the only woman I held in my arms tonight was you, Naomi." He caught her gaze with his, imploring her to believe him. "Only you."

Naomi stared at Rick, not certain what to say. She wanted desperately to believe him.

But her own insecurities, after the way Andrew had left her, held her back. So she took the coward's way out, acting as if they were just friends instead of very nearly lovers. "I'm glad I could be here for you."

His gaze searched hers. "Do you mind if I ask a question?"

She swallowed hard and shook her head. "I don't mind."

"How long have you been divorced?"

She shouldn't have been surprised he knew about her divorce. There weren't many secrets among the trauma surgery group. Since he'd bared his soul about his marriage, she figured it was only fair for him to know about her past. "Two years."

The same amount of time since his wife had died. She grimaced at the irony.

"Were you married long?"

"Not really. Just a few years." She could feel the heat of his intense gaze. "Andrew didn't like the long hours I worked either. I think, in all honesty, he liked the idea of being married to a physician rather than the reality of it."

"You didn't have any children?"

"I had a miscarriage." She didn't want to go into detail about her infertility problems. "Unfortunately, I suffered a lot of bleeding afterwards, to the point they needed to do a D and C and give me two blood transfusions."

Rick frowned. "Scary. Thank heavens you're all right."

His caring attitude touched her heart. Andrew had been more worried about the fact that she'd probably never have another baby than about her physical and emotional state. "Yes, I'm fine."

It was on the tip of her tongue to tell him the rest, to trust that he wouldn't react like Denis and Andrew had, but she glanced at her watch and realized it was getting late. She needed to be up early to be in the PICU. "Thanks for dinner, but I think I should probably get home."

"I understand." Rick stood and began gathering up their discarded white cardboard containers.

She jumped up to help. When their fingers touched as they both reached for the bag, she found herself wishing she hadn't stopped his kiss.

If she hadn't, the night might be ending very differently.

"What time would you like me to pick you up on Friday?" Rick asked, as he tossed the empty containers in the garbage.

Huh? Friday? For a moment her mind went completely blank. Then she remembered. The conference. Their train ride to Chicago. "How about nine? I know it's early, but I planned on taking the ten o'clock train, just to make sure I have plenty of time to prepare and get settled for our presentation at six."

"I'll pick you up at nine o'clock in the morning, then." He walked her to the door.

"Good night, Rick." To avoid any awkwardness, she reached up and brushed a light kiss on his cheek. "Take care."

"Naomi?" He caught her hand and pulled her close, pressing a firm kiss against her lips. "That's better. Good night."

Breathless, she could only nod, before turning and going outside. She fumbled for her keys, finally managing to get her car door open.

Her mouth tingled from his kiss. As she drove home, she couldn't help but smile.

In a few days, they'd be in Chicago at the annual trauma conference. Alone. For the entire weekend.

Anything was possible.

Friday morning Naomi overslept. She rushed through her shower, and then stood and stared at her closet, trying to figure out what to wear. She shook her head at her own foolishness, acting like a girl going out on her first date.

This wasn't a date. Technically, the dinner they'd shared at Rick's condo might have been a date. But this was a professional conference.

As much as she thought of nothing but spending the weekend with Rick, she knew she needed to get a grip. She was letting her imagination run away with her.

When her doorbell rang at a quarter after nine, she

went to answer it. Rick flashed a sheepish smile. "I'm late."

She grinned at him. "That's okay. I was running late myself." Opening the door, she stepped back to let him in. "I was just going to review my presentation, but I can wait until we're on the train. Just give me a minute to shut down my computer and I'll be ready to go."

"Sounds good." He gazed around her house with obvious interest, despite her rather eclectic taste in furnishings. "Nice place. Have you been here long?"

She lifted a shoulder as she shut off her computer. "About four years. I kept the house after my divorce."

He nodded. "Good choice. It's nice, homey."

"Exactly." She was pleased he saw what she did, a house that was really a home. Comfortable furniture, landscape paintings, lots of windows. Not the showcase mansion her ex-husband had wanted. "Thanks. I like it, too."

As she packed her laptop into its carrying case, Rick wandered into her kitchen and then back out again, reaching for the case as she zipped it closed. "All set?"

"Yes." She didn't argue when he slung her computer case over his shoulder. But they fought for a minute over the small overnight case.

Rick won the tussle. "I have it."

She wanted to protest, but figured he'd only ignore her anyway. Just like that first day, when he'd paid for her lunch, treating her like a woman, not like a colleague.

Funny, this time it didn't bother her as much.

He stored her suitcase and computer in his trunk. She frowned when she noticed his sleek, black BMW. "Are you sure you're all right with leaving your car at the station?"

"Sure. It's only a car."

But an expensive one. If it were her car, she wouldn't leave it at the train station. Pushing aside her apprehension, she climbed into the passenger seat.

The ride to the station didn't take long. They arrived just in time to board. Once they were settled in their adjacent seats and the train had begun to move, Rick gestured to her laptop. "Let's review the presentation."

She pulled out her computer and turned it on, sharply aware of the tangy scent of his aftershave as he leaned closer to see her computer screen. She angled the computer toward him, wetting her lips and trying to ignore her reaction as she walked him through her slide presentation.

"Excellent," he said in a low, admiring tone when she'd finished. "Frank's presentation picks up where yours leaves off."

She nodded, opening another file. "He sent it to me. Did you make any changes? If not, I can simply add yours to mine to make the hand-off smoother."

"I did actually update a few things," he admitted. "But I'll send the slides to you via e-mail once we get to the hotel, so you can put the two presentations together."

"No problem." An awkward silence fell. With the little bit of work out of the way, there was nothing more to do, so she shut her laptop down and packed it away. "Are you staying all weekend for the conference?"

"Yes." He shot her a surprised look. "Aren't you?"

She hid her relief. "Yes. I just wasn't sure if you were able to do the same."

"I took over Frank's reservation." Sitting as they were, side by side, their knees were touching. Even though they were no longer sharing the laptop screen, he stayed right next to her. "Maybe we can stop for lunch when we get to Chicago."

A lunch date? No, this was a conference, remember? Yet it felt far more like a date than a conference.

Before she could agree to lunch, a sharp whistle blew for a prolonged time. The train lurched, metal wheels screeching loudly as the train tried to stop.

Suddenly they were airborne, screams echoing throughout the train as their coach jumped off the tracks and crashed sideways, sliding over the rough terrain.

CHAPTER TEN

RICK carefully unclenched his muscles when the coaches stopped moving. Screams echoed but seemingly far away as if coming from other coaches. Shoving a suitcase off him, he stood and looked around for Naomi.

His breath froze when he saw her lying a few feet away, wedged between a suitcase and the roof of the train. For interminable seconds he relived the past all over again. He climbed over a seat, dropping to her side, and felt for a pulse. "Naomi?"

Her eyelids fluttered open and his breath left his lungs in a relieved whoosh. "Rick?"

A wave a relief hit hard. She was alive. Thank heavens she was alive. "Are you hurt?" He pushed the suitcase away, examining her for himself. No blood. Thank heavens there was no obvious sign of injury. "Can you move your arms and legs for me? We need to get out of here."

"Yes." She proved she was all right by testing her limbs, then gingerly sitting up. "What about the others? Is anyone else hurt? We need to help the victims."

They did need to offer aid to others, but not until he was convinced she was all right. Naomi was pale, but otherwise seemed fine. Her strength never ceased to amaze him. She pulled herself together and looked around. He couldn't ignore the others any longer. There were a few other people in their coach, and he was glad to see they were moving about. "Everyone all right?" he called, looking at each of the dazed occupants.

Most nodded in agreement, a few looked shocked. Rick glanced around, wondering how they were going to get out. "We might have to climb up through a window."

"You'll have to give me a boost." Naomi followed his gaze. "Hurry, I'm sure there are injured passengers."

She was right. Judging by the screams and crying, there were injured people needing assistance. Feeling the same sense of urgency, he used a small computer case to break through a window, ducking when glass rained down on his head. He tossed a blanket over the edge, and then gave Naomi a boost up and through. He followed her out, grateful to see many people already milling about outside, although several were locals, coming to offer help.

The extent of the train wreckage was sobering. A large section of the train was on its side, well off the track, bent coaches looking like crushed aluminum cans. The derailed train could have been dropped out of the sky in a heap of twisted metal. The worst damage appeared to be the front portion of the train, where a plume of black smoke could be seen rising from the wreckage. He and Naomi headed in that direction.

Hysterical sobs caught his attention a little way down. He stopped to investigate, but Naomi kept going. He wanted to insist she stay with him, but splitting up to share their expertise was smart. At least, it was the right thing to do.

A man came through the top window, looking frantic. "I'm a doctor," Rick informed him, climbing up to meet him. "You have injured people in there?"

"Yes, a woman." The young man, in his early twenties, looked relieved to have help. "This way," he said, disappearing back down through the window.

Rick followed him down into the coach. A woman was bleeding profusely from a head injury, babbling somewhat incoherently. "Help me. Help me!"

"Shh, I'm here, its okay." Rick understood the emotional effects of trauma, and he dropped to his knees beside her, talking in a low reassuring voice as he examined her more closely. The wound bleeding profusely was a huge cut in her forehead, above her right eye and extending down to the bone. He didn't have a first-aid kit or anything to use to help staunch the blood. He turned toward the young man who'd followed him over. "Open one of these suitcases, get me something to use as a dressing."

"Do you hurt anywhere else?" he asked, trying to get the woman's attention away from the copious amount of blood drenching her face, hands and shirt. "How about your neck? Your arms and legs?"

"Just my head." Her cries had quietened down to hiccuping sobs.

"Here." The young man pushed a soft cotton T-shirt into his hands.

Rick used the shirt to help wrap the woman's head. "You're fine, head wounds always bleed a lot. You'll need stitches, though, so we need to get you out of here."

His calm approach helped to defuse the situation. After he had the woman's head dressed, he turned to the young man. "I need you to help get her out of here. Is anyone else injured here?"

The young man nodded and dropped his voice. "There's a guy toward the front, I…uh, think he might be dead."

"I'll take a look," Rick promised. "You help get her out of here."

Rick left the woman in the hands of the young man and went to investigate. Sure enough, there was an elderly man, who lay at an awkward angle toward the front of the coach. He felt for a pulse, but wasn't surprised when he didn't find one. The angle of the man's head indicated he had probably died on impact with a broken neck.

He moved from that coach to the next. He found another passenger with two broken legs and a minor head injury. After splinting the victim's legs the best he could with what he could find, he continued moving through the wreckage, feeling as if he'd been dropped into the midst of a horrific war zone.

Sirens, dozens and dozens of sirens filled the air, bringing emergency help to the scene. A medical helicopter hovered, looking for a place to land.

Most of the injuries fell into one extreme or the

other. He saw several people with minor injuries. He also found another dead victim, with no outward obvious signs of injury. Either the woman had died of bleeding into her brain or possibly of a heart attack during the crash. As he couldn't help the dead victims, he left them where he found them and kept searching for more injured passengers.

When he reached the front of the train, the twisted coaches were so badly crushed, he couldn't get into them. Then he stumbled on Naomi. "Are you all right?" he asked, putting his arm around her shoulders.

She nodded and leaned against him, her eyes shadowed. "The train hit a car sitting on the tracks. No one knows why the car was there, but the driver didn't make it."

He wasn't surprised, considering the extent of the wreckage. "Did you find many seriously injured?"

"Not too many." A ghost of a smile played over her features. "Luckily, the children seemed to fare better than the adults. Except for these first few cars, where I couldn't even get in to see if anyone survived."

"I know." He'd tried to get in as well, but the twisted metal didn't leave any opening. Paramedics had flooded the scene, taking the pressure off them but, still, he and Naomi kept searching, neither of them willing to stand around doing nothing when there might be an unconscious victim buried in the wreckage.

Hours passed and the area around the derailed train slowly emptied of people as the injured were taken to local hospitals for treatment. Now that the rescue crews were on the scene, loaded with equipment, their assistance wasn't necessary. In fact, they were politely thanked for their efforts and escorted out of the way.

"We'd better call the hotel and let the conference convenors know we're not coming," Rick mused, when he and Naomi stood on the fringes of the scene.

"What do you mean, not coming?" Naomi looked at her watch. "It's only two-thirty in the afternoon. We still have time to get to Chicago."

Stunned, he stared at her. "Are you serious? After everything you've been through, you still want to go?"

"We're not hurt," she pointed out. "I hate to let the conference team down. What will they do if we don't give our presentation?"

"But we don't have our luggage or your computer." He didn't know why he was surprised at her persistence. He should have known better. At the stubborn glint in her eye, he sighed. "I guess we can borrow a computer from the hotel, and go online to retrieve our presentation."

"Of course we can." Naomi glanced around. "Now, if we could just get a ride out of here. Do you think one of these cops would call us a taxi?"

Three and a half hours later, they were standing on the stage in front of the podium, ready to make their presentation. The crowd was huge: at least five hundred people were seated in the hotel ballroom. He watched as Naomi gave her portion of the presentation with cool professionalism, no sign of their earlier crisis evident on her features. They both wore new clothes purchased from the mall conveniently located adjacent to the hotel. Naomi finished speaking, then handed over to him.

He went through Frank's slides, with a few of his own tossed in, giving the detailed results of their research study. When he'd finished, he stepped back and took questions.

And then it was over. The audience clapped, signaling the end. They'd done it. Despite surviving a train crash, they'd managed to pull off a presentation that hadn't been half-bad without anyone, except the conference coordinator, knowing the difference.

He and Naomi returned to their rooms, spacious suites located right next to each other. He paused outside her door. "Are you hungry? We never managed to have lunch."

She flashed a wan smile. "I am, but I'm not sure if I'm up to going downstairs to the restaurant. I think I'd rather just eat in my room."

"How about if I order room service for two?" Rick offered, knowing just how she felt. Going to the restaurant didn't appeal to him either. Although, after everything that happened, he wouldn't blame her if she wasn't in the mood for an intimate meal either. "The special of the evening is grilled swordfish, if you like seafood."

Her eyes widened, betraying a tiny flare of desire. His heart thudded when she nodded. "Perfect." She used her key card to open her door. "Just give me a few minutes and I'll be over."

His body tightened with a surge of heat intermixed with anticipation. "I'll be waiting."

Rick's suite, like hers, overlooked the scenic view of Lake Michigan. The living room was separate from the bedroom, but she still felt awkward being there in his personal space, so she crossed over to the balcony and stepped outside.

He joined her, handing her a glass of wine. "Beautiful, isn't it?"

"Very." She accepted the wine, and took a small sip even though she knew it would go straight to her head. The events of the day had been traumatic, but the horror dwindled away in the peacefulness of the night.

She took solace in knowing most of the injured had survived the crash, except for the people in the coaches closest to the front of the train. After it was all said and done, the number of deaths could have been much worse than the eighteen reported by the media.

"Dinner will be up shortly." He touched the rim of his glass to hers in a silent toast. "To us."

Her lips curved in a smile. Was it wrong to celebrate life, after experiencing such tragedy? Somehow she didn't think so. "To us. We did it."

His gaze was dark, intense. "You were amazing."

She shook her head. "Not just me. Both of us." Soft music played in the background, from the radio he'd turned on. The cool breeze off the lake made her shiver. He noticed and stepped closer, coming up behind her to cradle her in a gesture of sweet protectiveness.

She leaned back into his embrace, glad to be there with Rick rather than sitting alone in her room. When he pressed a kiss to the side of her neck, she shivered again, but not from the cold. The area just below her ear was one of her erogenous zones.

A knock at the door interrupted them. Reluctantly she turned as Rick let her go long enough to cross over to the door. A hotel employee wheeled in a small table, set for two.

"Do you want to eat on the patio?" Rick asked.

"That would be lovely." She didn't care about the coolness of the night. With Rick seated across from her, she suspected his smoldering gaze would keep her warm.

They ate slowly, leisurely, enjoying the moment as if in complete agreement they had all night. The food tasted wonderful, although she had to admit the sensual atmosphere may have helped add to the flavor.

She kept the conversation light, not willing to ruin the mood. "Do you enjoy traveling? At least, when there isn't a train crash?"

He chuckled, a low raspy sound that curled her toes. "Yes, I like to travel. It's one of the best perks of this job, in my opinion. Being a guest lecturer has its advantages. I've been as far as Tokyo without having to pay out of my own pocket."

"This was my first time, being a guest lecturer," she confided, smoothing a finger down the side of her wineglass. She gave a self-deprecating laugh. "I guess that's why I was so determined to come."

"There will be more chances," he said, in a tone that held a note of promise. "But next time maybe you should fly, instead of taking the train."

She let out a small laugh. Sitting back with a contented sigh, she tipped her face up to the breeze. "This was a wonderful idea, eating outside. Just what I needed. Thank you."

"You're welcome." He pushed back his chair and

stood. "Naomi, I'm not ready for the evening to end. Will you stay? At least for a while?"

Her pulse skipped, and she knew what he was really asking her. After the heated kiss they'd shared at his condo, she couldn't deny she wanted that closeness again. When he came to stand beside her and held out his hand, she didn't hesitate but placed her palm against his.

"Yes. I'll stay."

He drew her into his arms, dipped his head and covered her mouth with his. The kiss wasn't tentative or gentle, but hot and demanding, as if he was at the end of his patience. Every cell in her body responded to his touch, celebrating life.

He kissed her until she thought she might die from the sensation. Then he found that same ultra-sensitive spot beneath her ear, and she clung to his shoulder, unable to hold back a tiny moan of pleasure. She caught her breath when his teeth lightly scraped the curve of her neck.

Drowning. She was drowning in pleasure but she didn't want a life-preserver. She only wanted Rick.

She could feel his hard length pressing against her. Her fingers fumbled with his shirt and he tugged her toward the bedroom. It took her a moment to think. "Ah, do you have protection?"

"Yes." His hungry gaze searched hers, as if looking for reassurance. Had he thought she'd be upset? Far from it.

"Good," she whispered. Knowing he'd actually planned this, it only made her want him more. He kissed her again, then swung her into his arms and carried her the short distance to his king-sized bed.

Stepping back from the bed, he held her gaze as he peeled off his clothes. Her mouth went dry as he took off his shirt, and she reached up to unbutton her blouse. His dark gaze fell to the shadowed cleavage as she bared herself to his hungry gaze.

"You're so beautiful." He dropped his pants and his boxers, not at all embarrassed by his nudity. He kissed the valley between her breasts as he helped her to get rid of the rest of her clothing. Every part of her body was lovingly caressed by his fingers or his mouth, and she was more than ready when he gently eased her legs apart and, after sheathing himself, thrust deep.

She gasped, sheer pleasure nearly blinding her. "Naomi." He whispered her name as he pulled back, then thrust again. "I've wanted you for so long."

Unable to speak, she lost herself in the dizzying sensation, the mounting ache and the need to come driving her to meet each of his thrusts with one of her own.

His muscles tensed and he lifted her hips, urging her to take more. "Naomi, please. More. Please…"

She knew what he was asking for and let herself go in reckless abandon. Pleasure burst like a kaleidoscope of color in her mind and her body spasmed against his as he followed her over the edge, clutching her close, murmuring her name.

They stayed entwined together for a long time. When she made herself move, to find the comfort of her own bed, he raised his head. "Stay with me."

She couldn't deny his request when she badly wanted to spend the night with him. "All right."

He made love to her again hours later and this time there was no urgency—at least, not at first, only at the thrilling end.

Shaken by what they'd shared, she stroked the damp skin of his back and held back the words of love that trembled on her lips.

CHAPTER ELEVEN

THE next morning, satisfied if not totally rested, Naomi slipped back to her own suite to shower and change her clothes, as the conference started at eight. Rick was waiting for her when she opened her door and stepped into the hall.

"Good morning." His lazy smile was contagious. "Figured we may as well go down together."

"Why not?" She fell into step beside him.

They sat together, sharing a breakfast of juice, fruit and bagels. The ballroom was just as crowded today, their shoulders touching as they sat side by side through several very interesting presentations. Naomi's mind was only partially on the new surgical techniques they were discussing because she found Rick's presence distracting. Especially when he leaned over to whisper in her ear, offering to refill her coffee-cup or fetch her more water.

There was no sign that he regretted their night together. Or that their time together was over. She wished she knew what exactly he was thinking. She decided not to overanalyze things, but to be more like Rick and go with the flow.

Not easy for a control-freak trauma surgeon, but she gave it her best shot.

At lunch, he didn't head into the restaurant with all the others. "Let's go outside."

The sun was shining and it took a few minutes for their eyes to adjust to the brightness. She looked up and down Michigan Avenue. "Where to?"

"The Navy Pier," he said, with a tug on her hand. "It's way too nice to waste the entire day indoors."

He was right. They ordered giant hot dogs from an outside hotdog stand, and ate as they wandered along the lakeshore. Instead of going back inside to the afternoon sessions of the conference, they decided to play hookey and go to the planetarium instead. Naomi had never been inside the planetarium and found the reclining seats and the dozens of stars overhead awesome.

For dinner they stopped at a little restaurant right on the Pier. He took several calls from some of their surgeon colleagues who'd heard about the train crash on the news, and she listened as Rick gave them his abbreviated version of what had happened.

After dinner, they walked hand in hand back to the hotel. They went straight to his room and, holding her close, he unlocked his door.

She held back, lifting a questioning brow. "You're making a big assumption," she teased.

His smile faded, his expression turning serious. "I know. Will you stay?"

How could she refuse? "Yes. I'll stay."

They made love again, only this time, their protection failed. When he realized what had happened, Rick propped himself up on his elbow and looked down at her with a worried expression. "Naomi, are you on the Pill?"

She mentally counted back and realized it had been five days since her cycle had ended. "No, but the timing isn't right." She licked her suddenly dry lips, realizing she needed to trust him by telling him everything. "And you should know, according to my doctor, my chances of conceiving at all are very slim."

He frowned and tightened his arm around her. "I'm sorry. But I thought you had a miscarriage?"

"I did. That's when I discovered that my bouts of endometriosis had left a significant amount of scar tissue." Since she'd come this far, she may as well tell him the rest. "Andrew wanted out of our marriage, not just because of my schedule but because of my possible infertility."

"He's a fool." Rick's gaze was warm, filled with compassion. As if he knew just what she needed, he leaned over and kissed her, accepting her for the way she was, imperfections and all. Soon their kiss led to more, causing them to be late for their conference session the following morning.

The part of the program they did hear was informative but once again after the session Rick led her outside for lunch.

"This is wonderful," she murmured, gazing up at the sunny sky, basking in the cool breeze off the lake. "It won't be easy to go back to work after this."

"Speaking of work, I think we should stay an extra day," Rick said. "Neither one of us is on duty tomorrow so there's no reason we couldn't stay tonight and take the train home first thing Monday morning."

He was right—there was no reason not to stay another day. Being away like this was exactly what she'd needed after the stressful weeks of working extra shifts to cover her colleagues not to mention having been in a train wreck.

Making love with Rick had been very relaxing and fun. And she was thrilled she'd told him her deepest fear and he hadn't left.

She realized he was staring at her, his gaze solemn as he waited for her answer. While going home might be the smart thing to do, she quite honestly didn't want their time together to end. Was he planning to continue their relationship now that they'd become intimate? Hope filled her heart. "I'd like that."

"Good." He grinned, looking more relaxed than she'd ever seen him. "I thought we'd have dinner somewhere nice—there's a restaurant at the top of the John Hancock Center. I hear they have an awesome view."

"Sounds perfect."

They attended the afternoon sessions, but Naomi's mind wasn't on the program. The way Rick often caught her gaze, she had to think he wasn't totally engrossed by the knowledge being shared either.

"We have dinner reservations at the Signature Room for seven," he told her after their mid-afternoon break. "I'm going to need to make a few phone calls after the presentation, but I'll pick you up at six-thirty. Shouldn't take long to get across town."

"All right." She didn't mind a few hours alone—in

fact, she hoped to hit a few of the shops again before they closed. Leaving their luggage in the train wreck was a good excuse to update her wardrobe.

Luckily, she found what she was looking for right away. A sleek red dress that hugged her torso but flared gently just above her knees. The color was good on her, with her dark hair and pale skin. Although the bridge of her nose and her cheeks were pink from the hours they'd spent walking in the sun.

There was no denying how she hoped the evening would end, right back in Rick's arms. She thought of their failed protection. As much as they'd spent hours making love, being together, they hadn't really talked about the future.

Tonight at dinner? Maybe. But she was also hesitant to rush him. She knew without asking that Rick hadn't been with a woman since his wife and daughter had died. Two years was a long time. He obviously wanted her physically, but emotionally was a whole different matter.

So much for not being a rebound romance, she thought with a grimace at her reflection in the mirror.

Rick knocked at her door at precisely six-thirty.

With one last glance, she smoothed a hand over her dress and turned to the door. Rick was dressed in the dark blue suit and red tie he'd worn for the presentation, and he exuded a masculine attraction that made her mouth go dry.

Although, really, he looked good no matter what he wore, rumbled scrubs, casual jeans or a nice suit.

"You're beautiful, Naomi." His greeting was low, husky.

"Thanks." She stepped out of her room, making sure she had her room key card before closing the door behind her.

Rick put his hand in the small of her back as they walked toward the elevators. "I have a taxi waiting for us out front."

He seemed to touch her constantly, holding her hand or putting his arm around her waist. She had no memory of the taxi ride to the Sears Tower John Hancock building, but the elevator ride to the ninety-fifth floor was interesting. Her ears popped halfway up and she had to swallow to get them to pop again so she could hear.

The Signature Room restaurant was spectacular, with floor-to-ceiling windows that displayed a breath-taking view of the lake. Dark wood with chrome accents gave the interior a luxurious aura.

"This way," the maître d' led them to an isolated table right next to the window. "Are you celebrating a special event this evening?" he asked as he handed them leather-bound menus.

"No," she answered quickly, feeling rather awkward at the assumption of the maître d'. "We're in town for a conference and heard this is a great place to have dinner."

"Welcome." He flashed them both a smile. "I hope you enjoy your evening."

Rick didn't say anything as the maître d' melted away.

Hyperaware of the silence, she stared at her menu, hoping her thoughts weren't written all over her face. After a few seconds she gave her head a little shake and forced herself to pay attention. Food. She needed to choose something to eat.

She stayed with fish, grilled tuna this time. Rick opted for steak. They shared a bottle of red wine.

"Frank called. He'll be coming back to work next week," Rick informed her when they were alone again.

"Great news." She was a little disappointed at how Rick had reverted back to talking about work. "I hope he takes it easy for a while now."

"He will. His wife has been on his case big time about changing his eating and exercising habits."

She smiled, imagining tiny Hilda taking on her husband Frank, who stood six feet tall with wide shoulders and had a head full of white hair. She'd often wondered how his thick fingers could do such intricate surgery. "I bet she has."

"We also have to start interviewing for the fellowship position," Rick continued. "I'm starting to screen qualified candidates. I'd like most of the faculty to help perform interviews, along with some key nursing leadership, of course."

More work. She hid a sigh and sipped her wine. "I'll help interview if need be."

"Great. We want to get the best possible candidates to take jobs with us. I'd really like to turn our trauma program around."

Turn the program around? Why? There wasn't anything wrong with it to begin with that she could see. Hadn't they already had a great level-one trauma re-verification visit?

Unless Rick was really telling her something else. Like subtly reinforcing the fact that he was still her boss.

And maybe hinting that their intimate relationship would end after tonight.

Her fingers tightened on the wineglass. After the wonderful nights they'd shared, she just couldn't believe this might be all Rick would allow them to have. Reminding herself not to overreact, she forced herself to relax and gazed out at the calming view of Lake Michigan.

She didn't get a chance to change the subject because one of the conference attendees recognized them and came over to chat. Dr Stolansky asked Rick several questions, only leaving when their food arrived.

Her tuna was delicious, but the romantic mood of the evening had fizzled out. She kept the conversation light, rather than delving into a deep, emotional conversation about the future.

Coward, she mentally chided herself.

After dinner they returned to the hotel. She half expected Rick to suggest they call it a night, each going back to their own rooms, but he surprised her.

"Your room or mine?" he asked, when they reached his door.

She bit her lip, assailed by indecision. Logically, she knew she should stop things right now, before she became more emotionally involved than she already was. But at the same time Rick's dark eyes promised passionate pleasure she longed for.

"I don't know," she confessed. "Rick—"

He interrupted her with a kiss, hauling her close, not giving her a chance to think. To breathe.

To refuse.

Suddenly they were in his room, making their way to his bed. He didn't stop, but there a note of desperation in his kiss, in the way his hands caressed her, as if he was trying to memorize every curve, every hollow, every inch of her skin.

He somehow managed to kiss her doubts away, especially when he kissed a path from her breasts to her belly and lower to the moistness between her thighs, replacing the doubt with a passion so intense she thought she might die of the pleasure.

It wasn't until later, much later, that the doubts returned.

Rick had known he'd have regrets the next morning, but hadn't anticipated how sharply they'd slash his heart.

Naomi slipped from his bed early, making her way back to her own room. He should have stopped her.

Instead, he let her go.

He closed his eyes against the wave of pain. It was for the best. This weekend had been like a mini-vacation, but now it was time to get back to reality.

Unable to go back to sleep, he got up and took a shower. Afterward he dressed and packed his new clothing in the new suitcase he'd purchased in the mall.

When he couldn't stall any longer, he went out to knock on Naomi's door.

She opened it and smiled, but her smile didn't quite reach her eyes. She indicated he should come in. He could see her suitcase was open on the bed. "I'm almost ready."

The door closed behind him with a loud thud. He realized they couldn't leave until they'd talked. "Naomi, I'm sorry."

"Don't." Her harsh tone caught him off guard, and she must have noticed his reaction because she softened her tone. "Look, I know you're worried about being my boss, but surely there are exceptions to the rule. They can't just get rid of me, it's not as if there are tons of pediatric trauma surgeons available to take my place."

Exceptions to the rule? Dating subordinates. Realizing what she meant, his heart squeezed in his chest. She'd told him she wasn't a woman who could settle for a quick fling.

And he hadn't been looking for anything more.

Still wasn't looking for anything more.

He cared about her. Couldn't have made love to her if he didn't. Yet he hadn't been a good husband to Gabrielle and Naomi had already been through one bad marriage.

They needed to step back, to really think about this. He couldn't just jump into another relationship. He tried to make her understand. "Naomi, I don't know that I'm ready for more. I can't think about the future."

She dropped her gaze and he knew he was hurting her. "I see."

He doubted she did when he was having trouble figuring it out himself. "I've already lost one family. I can't even think of having another." He lifted his shoulder in a helpless shrug. "I'm sorry."

"So am I." She turned her back on him, jammed some last-minute bathroom articles into her suitcase and then zipped the cover closed. He could tell she was angry and upset, but didn't know what to say or what to do to make it better.

His body had loved every minute they'd spent together. But even last night at dinner he'd known he'd made a mistake. Not just because of their work relationship but because Naomi deserved more than he had to offer.

She set the suitcase on the floor with a thump. "I'm sorry for your loss, Rick, I really am. But you were lucky to love two very special people." The brittle expression in her eyes sliced deep. "The only man I ever loved never loved me back."

He ached for her. He'd never meant to hurt her. Naomi deserved better than a guy like him. "Your ex was a fool."

"Really?" She met his gaze head on, silently challenging him. "Then so are you. Excuse me, but I really need to be alone right now. I'll catch my own ride back to Milwaukee."

She brushed past him, pulling her rolling suitcase behind her as she left the hotel room. He stepped back, allowing her go, knowing she needed space.

But the guilt wouldn't leave him alone. Because Naomi was right.

She was the best thing that had happened to him in a long time. And he'd let her walk away.

He was a fool.

* * *

Being apart from Naomi was more difficult than Rick had realized. He found himself thinking about her constantly, wondering if she was all right. For the first time in months he didn't think at all about the past but actually started envisioning a future.

Because of Naomi.

He missed her. Missed working with her. The camaraderie they'd shared during the train crash. Having fun. Making love.

Seeing her at the hospital was pure torture. A situation with Dirk being accused of negligence took up most of his time over the next few weeks. But sometimes, late at night, he'd think of Naomi and wonder.

Was she right?

Was he being selfish, holding back his love?

He cared about Naomi, deeply. She was a wonderful person and a great surgeon. But love wasn't something he could easily allow himself to feel. And he'd loved Gabrielle once, but that hadn't made him a great husband.

How could he avoid the mistakes of the past?

His sister could tell something was wrong. "What's up with you lately?" she asked one evening when he came over to babysit Lizzy while Jess went out on a date. "You were doing so much better and now you seem down in the dumps again."

He had been doing better, at least when he had been with Naomi. Of course, the situation with Dirk hadn't helped much either. "I'm fine," he lied. "Tell me about your date. Who is this guy?"

She flushed. "His name is Steve Sites. It's not a big

deal. We're just having dinner. He's a teacher at the high school."

"A teacher?" Rick was surprised. "I don't think you've mentioned him before."

She toyed with the strap of her purse. "He's relatively new. He was recruited to teach math and to be the new head football coach. He's been tutoring Lizzy."

Good for Lizzy, but football coach? "You don't like sports," he reminded her.

Jess shrugged and raised a brow. "I can learn."

He hoped his sister wasn't going to be hurt by this guy Steve, but it was only dinner. His sister certainly deserved to have some fun, especially as she didn't get out much. Being a single mother wasn't easy.

"Have fun," he told her, trying not to remember how his plan to have fun in Chicago had backfired in a big way.

"I will." She kissed Lizzy on the top of the head before leaving.

He and Lizzy watched the latest kids' movie, but his thoughts weren't on the film. Instead, he found himself wondering what Naomi was doing on a Saturday night. Had she decided to move on with her life? Was she right now going out with that guy, Jeff?

He shouldn't begrudge her happiness, but the thought of Naomi sharing an intimate meal with Jeff made him feel sick.

He sat up, realizing he didn't want to give up. Not yet. Even though he hadn't been looking for a relationship, he'd managed to find himself entangled in one anyway.

Maybe they could try again, but take things slowly.

See if this was something he could do or not. If she'd let him. They needed to talk. Soon.

Unfortunately, their schedules kept them apart, especially as they ended up covering most of Dirk's shifts during the investigation. It seemed like every time he saw her, she wasn't alone.

Finally, Rick stumbled on her sitting in the back conference room, her head down on her folded arms, as if she was totally exhausted.

"Hey, are you all right?" he asked in concern.

Naomi lifted her head, her expression going blank when she saw him. "I'm fine. Was there something you wanted?"

Not the most welcoming opening in the world, but a start. "Yes. You're off at five, aren't you?" Without waiting for her to nod, he continued, "I was hoping we could get together for dinner. I think…we should talk."

Even before he'd finished speaking she was shaking her head. "I can't, sorry. I'm really exhausted. Maybe another time?"

"Sure." Her remote attitude bothered him. She acted as if she couldn't care less if they got together or not. But the lines of fatigue etched in her features couldn't be denied. "I'll cover your next call shift. You need to catch up on some sleep."

"I'm fine," she repeated, rising to her feet. "See you later, Rick."

His heart thudded when she left without a backward glance.

Naomi obviously wasn't interested. And he had no one to blame but himself.

CHAPTER TWELVE

SHE was pregnant.

Naomi stared down at the white test strip, hardly able to believe what she was seeing. She blinked several times, but this wasn't a dream. No matter how long she gazed at the test strip, the red plus sign remained as clear as day.

Stunned, she tried to get her head around the news. How could this have happened? Their protection had only failed once. The timing hadn't been right. And even if the timing had been right, her doctor had explained about the scar tissue and how it would affect her ability to become pregnant.

With all the strikes against her, how could she have gotten pregnant at the wrong time?

She swallowed hard, putting a hand to her stomach. The overwhelming exhaustion. The never-ending nausea. The constant going to the bathroom.

Everything made sense now.

The baby was a miracle. Despite her upset stomach, she grinned like a fool. A true miracle. The thrill of excitement faded.

Rick. How on earth was she going to tell him?

Her knees gave out and she sat down, feeling dizzy. After the way they'd parted in Chicago, she didn't think he'd take the news well. He wasn't ready to think about the future. He wasn't ready for a family.

Maybe she should wait. It was too early to know if this pregnancy would last any longer than last time. Maybe she shouldn't tell him until she was sure she wouldn't lose the baby.

Good plan. She would wait. See what the doctor said after her first appointment. For all she knew, the pregnancy might not be viable.

Except she felt different.

During her first, brief pregnancy, she hadn't felt so sick. Or so tired she could fall asleep in the middle of the noisy cafeteria at lunchtime. And for sure she hadn't felt so moody.

These symptoms were all caused by an increase in hormones. So the fact she felt so awful was really a good thing. Right? Right.

Except she didn't feel as happy as she'd imagined she would. Because even though this child had certainly been conceived out of love on her part, what she really wanted was the whole package.

A husband. A family.

Everything Rick wasn't ready for.

Rick stared at the picture of Gabrielle and Sarah, their bright, sunny smiles no longer making him wish he'd been in the car with them when they'd died.

He forced himself to remember every wonderful, heart-wrenching moment they'd shared. In spite of how he and Gabrielle had argued at the end, they'd still also had lots of great times together. They'd both been thrilled to have a daughter.

Sarah's presence in their lives had been so short, but he cherished every memory. Even the not-so-good ones, the late-night feedings, the colicky episodes of nonstop crying. The time she'd scared them both by running a high fever. Even the difficult times had been wonderful.

Until he'd had Sarah, he'd never realized how much you could love your child.

Naomi's words had haunted him in the weeks they'd been apart. She was right—loving and losing the ones you loved was much better than to never have loved at all.

He had to admit he wouldn't have given up his short time with Gabrielle and Sarah for anything. And if he thought back, past the guilt, he realized not all of Gabrielle's issues had been his fault. She'd admitted as much. Still, he did have lingering regrets. He wished he'd spent more time with them. He wished he'd been a better husband and father. Maybe Gabrielle had been right and he should have been more involved in their lives. He firmly believed they would have found a way to work things out.

He would always miss them, but now the feeling was bittersweet rather than painful. Well-meaning people had tried to tell him how grief and mourning didn't last for ever, but he hadn't believed them. For so long the pain had been acute.

Now he went for days, weeks without even thinking about them. Or missing them. He'd finally moved on.

When his phone rang, he recognized Naomi's number. After not hearing from her in well over a month, he swiftly answered the phone on the first ring. "Hello?"

"Rick?"

Her voice was so soft he almost couldn't hear her. "Naomi? What is it?"

"I don't think I'll make my call shift tonight."

"Tell me what's wrong. Are you sick?" He didn't bother to hide his concern. Maybe he should drive over to check on her.

"Yeah, I…I guess. Normally I'd tough it out, but I honestly don't think I can work. I'm sorry to do this to you at the last minute."

"I'll cover your shift, don't worry about it." He tightened his grip on the phone, hating feeling helpless. "If there's anything else you need, though, let me know."

"I don't need…" She didn't finish her sentence and the way she hung up so abruptly caused him to stare at the phone in dismay.

There was something wrong. Every nerve in his body was screaming at him that something was wrong. Most of the trauma team didn't call in sick without a good reason. Was she seriously ill? Memories of Lizzy's food poisoning episode flashed into his mind.

He called Frank, asking him if he could cover Naomi's shift. He planned to go through the entire list of trauma surgeons if he had to, but luckily Frank came through for him.

"Sure, I'll cover her shift, no problem. All of you bailed me out during my heart troubles. And Naomi in particular recently covered me so that I could take Hilda away for the weekend."

That was Naomi, generous to a fault. She'd covered his shift for him, too. He wasn't surprised to discover she'd helped out the others.

"Thanks." With that problem solved, he called Naomi's number again. Only this time her phone rang and rang, eventually going to her answering-machine. He hung up without leaving a message.

Damn. He paced the length of his condo, trying to be patient. Yet he couldn't stand not knowing if she was really okay. Giving up, he whirled around, grabbed his keys from the kitchen counter and headed outside.

He wouldn't be happy until he'd seen Naomi for himself.

Naomi threw up, her stomach rejecting the chicken and rice dinner she'd eaten earlier. She stayed in the bathroom for a long time, hoping she wouldn't get sick again. Strangely enough, her stomach always felt better after it was empty. When she was certain the episode was over, she rinsed out her mouth and brushed her teeth, wincing when she caught a glimpse of her wan reflection in the mirror over the basin.

She looked awful. Pale, angular face, dark circles beneath her eyes, limp hair.

Was there something more serious wrong with her? For a moment she was plagued by doubts. She'd read up enough on pregnancy to know there was such a problem called hyperemesis, but she honestly didn't think she was quite to that stage. At least, not yet.

Although maybe she should call her doctor to make an appointment sooner rather than later.

She shuffled back into the kitchen to make herself more dry toast. She was starting to think she'd spend her entire pregnancy eating dry toast. Wasn't morning sickness supposed to be only in the mornings? Why on earth they called it morning sickness, when she felt lousy all day, even well into the evening, was beyond her.

There was a loud knock on her door. She frowned and went to answer it, doubly surprised to find Rick standing on her doorstep.

"What are you doing here?" She tried to read his expression, not easy after they hadn't talked for so long. "Did you change your mind about covering for me?"

"No, Frank's covering your shift." He didn't ask if he could come in but opened the screen door and stepped over the threshold. She backed up, allowing him to come in. "I'm here to see you. I was worried when you hung up on me."

"I didn't," she protested weakly, remembering her mad dash to the bathroom. "At least, not on purpose," she amended.

He closed the door behind him and pressed a hand to her forehead, as if to gauge whether she was running a fever. "You look awful," he said bluntly, and while she knew he was right—hadn't she thought the same thing herself?—his words still hurt. "Are you running a fever? Do you have other symptoms?"

"No fever." She stared at him, realizing she wasn't going to be able to hide the truth. Rick wasn't stupid.

If she continued to be sick for weeks on end, he'd know she wasn't suffering from a bug.

Besides, what if the others guessed? Debra Maloney had two children of her own, and would know right away she was pregnant.

Preparing herself for the worst, she gestured to the living-room sofa. "I'm glad you're here. Please, sit down."

"There's something really wrong with you, isn't there?" He didn't sit but lightly grabbed her arms, peering deep into her eyes. Her body responded to his light touch, starving for more after not being close to him for so long. "Sweetheart, you can tell me."

Sweetheart? She really wished that were true. Her stomach clenched, somersaulted and she wasn't sure if it was the nausea from the baby returning or the idea of confessing her condition to Rick.

"Naomi?" He gave her a light shake. "Please, tell me."

She licked her lips, tasting toothpaste. "Rick, I don't know how else to say this, but…I'm pregnant."

He blinked. The color drained from his face and his hands tightened on her shoulders. "What?"

"I'm pregnant. The weekend we spent in Chicago…" She didn't have to finish.

He let her go and took several steps backward, running his hands through his hair. Myriad expressions crossed his face—disbelief, doubt, confusion. "I thought you said the timing wasn't right?"

Maybe it was the overabundance of hormones swimming through her bloodstream but she immediately took offense. "I wasn't lying. The timing wasn't right. And I was told by my doctor I probably wouldn't conceive. And it's not my fault the condom broke!"

He held up a hand in surrender. "I'm sorry. I'm not accusing you of lying—it's just such a shock."

Yeah, no kidding. Her anger faded, and she smiled. "I know. But it's also a miracle, Rick. A true miracle."

He looked in shock, worse than after the train wreck. "Pregnant. I can't believe you're pregnant."

She had to be honest. "You need to know, this isn't a sure thing. I mean, I've been pregnant once before but lost the baby after eight weeks. I was going to wait to tell you, but I've been so tired and so sick, I figured you'd better know."

He still didn't say anything, obviously trying to absorb the news.

"I know you said you didn't want this but, Rick, we're having a baby." She silently urged him to be happy.

"A baby." The dazed, almost fearful expression in his eyes was not reassuring.

He turned away, scrubbing his hands over his face. "I'm sorry, but I think I'm still in shock. This may take me a while to absorb."

How did he think she'd felt, staring at that pregnancy test? But she tried to understand. Rising to her feet, she took a few steps toward the kitchen.

"Where are you going?" he asked.

She paused. "To get a glass of water. I'm thirsty."

He let out his breath on a sigh. "Sit down. I'll get it. Bedsides, I could use something myself."

Sensing he needed time alone to adjust, she sat back down. In spite of Rick's obvious shock, this was going better than she'd expected.

She placed a hand over her still-flat abdomen. Would he come to love his child with the same depth and intensity he'd loved Sarah? She hoped so.

Leaning her head back against the sofa, she closed her eyes on a wave of exhaustion. How could she be so tired? She'd slept in that morning and hadn't done anything remotely physical. Well, if you didn't count throwing up her dinner.

The toast seemed to be staying down this time, though. Maybe if things went well, she'd try some soup. The baby couldn't live on vitamins alone.

Rick seemed to be taking a long time in the kitchen. They needed to talk about immediate issues, like her position with the trauma program. If her all-day, constant nausea continued, she might have to change to a part-time status, at least until she was feeling better.

And she didn't want to resign from her position. Would Administration consider making an exception? She hoped so. Although she didn't want anyone accusing Rick of playing favorites.

She wanted to plan their future. She wanted a loving, caring family.

Rick. She wanted Rick.

She opened her eyes when she heard the heavy tread of Rick's footsteps. Surprised, she noticed his face was tight with anger. Then she noticed the brochure he clutched in one hand. With a sinking heart she remembered the New Life Clinic brochure she'd stuck on the front of her fridge with a magnet.

He thrust the crumpled paper under her nose. "What is this? Did you use me to get pregnant on purpose?"

CHAPTER THIRTEEN

RICK was so angry he could hardly see straight. While reaching for a glass, he'd noticed the brochure on the fridge. At first, he'd feared it was for some sort of abortion clinic. He had still been in shock over hearing about Naomi's pregnancy, but he'd never thought she wouldn't keep their baby.

After reading the brochure, he'd quickly realized it was quite the opposite.

Artificial insemination. He'd felt foolish. And gullible. She'd used him to get pregnant. Hell, maybe the baby wasn't even his.

"It's not what you think."

Sure. Right. Her eyes, wide with guilt told him it was exactly what he'd thought. A red haze blurred his vision. "Answer me. Did you plan to get pregnant?" He shook the brochure at her. "Plan to have a baby? Either by me or by artificial insemination?"

"Rick, I swear I didn't use you to get pregnant. I did go the clinic once, but I changed my mind while I was there. I didn't go through with the procedure. I know it looks bad, but this baby is yours. I wouldn't lie to you about something like this."

He had to look away from her earnest gaze because there was a tiny part of him that wanted to believe her.

And if he was honest, he'd admit she couldn't have planned for their protection to fail.

"Rick, I know you're shocked by all this but, believe me, I am, too." She stared at him. "I decided against raising a baby on my own. Because I wanted more."

He didn't know what to say. In Chicago she'd told him she wanted to continue their relationship. He was the one who had let her go.

Now she was pregnant.

He cared about Naomi. He'd opened his heart to her, shared his deepest emotions with her. But he'd only just become accustomed to the idea of starting over. He'd needed time, had wanted to go slowly. To explore what they might have.

A baby changed everything.

Tension tightened his chest. He didn't want to fail. As a husband or a father. Not again. He tossed the crumpled brochure on the living-room table. "I have to go."

"Just like that?" Her jaw dropped. "You're going to leave? Why? Because that's what you always do? Because you're not interested in having a child? Because you've already lost one?"

He stopped and turned to look at her, knowing he probably deserved to have his comments tossed back in his face.

"Do you think Gabrielle would like the way you've become?" she continued, obviously on a roll. "So emotionally cold and distant? Running away from true emotions? Maybe that was the real reason she was thinking of leaving you?"

He sucked in a harsh breath. Low blow. "How dare you blame me for grieving over my wife and child? You don't know anything about how I felt."

"I had a miscarriage." Her tone was defensive.

"It's not even close. To hold your daughter, to watch her grow and then to lose her." He stopped. Took another deep breath. "You know nothing." Blindly, he turned away.

"Rick, don't leave—not like this."

He had to leave. Before he said worse things he'd regret. "Don't worry, I'm not abandoning my child. I don't run out on my obligations."

"I don't want to be your obligation."

"Jess and I grew up without a father." He continued toward the door. "I'll be damned if I'll put my child through that."

Silence. He glanced back at her, realizing it was the first time she didn't have a snappy comeback. Her expression, full of empathy, caught him off guard.

He didn't want her sympathy. He needed to think. To figure out where they were going to go from here. Without another word, he turned and walked away.

Naomi sank back down onto the sofa when the front door closed behind Rick. Tears threatened, burning the back of her throat, and she buried her face in her hands, trying to hold them back.

But as her mind insisted on replaying Rick's angry accusations, a few tears leaked from the corners of her eyes, dampening her skin.

He thought she'd used him. Because of the New Life brochure. Why hadn't she tossed the stupid thing in the garbage? She should have thrown it away after her one and only failed visit.

Too late.

Her chest hurt with the effort to breathe. She struggled to remain calm. Rick wasn't going to simply leave. He just needed some time alone. The news of her pregnancy had been a major shock.

A flash of anger caught her off guard. She'd been shocked and stunned, too. She hadn't planned on getting pregnant.

He and his sister had been raised without a father. She hadn't known that. But things were clearer now that she knew. It explained so much. His protective attitude toward Jess. And Lizzy. His disparaging feelings toward the guy who had fathered Lizzy and left.

No wonder he'd reacted so strongly to the New Life brochure.

He wouldn't abandon her or their child.

But she wanted more than a sense of responsibility.

The pressure in her chest tightened and a wrenching sob broke free. He'd never forgive her. As much as she'd wanted a baby at first, she'd quickly learned that a baby alone wasn't really what she wanted at all. She'd stopped the procedure and left the clinic without planning to ever go back.

What she really wanted was a family. Rick and their own, miracle baby. Knowing she'd inadvertently sacrificed her relationship with Rick was almost too much to bear.

She's fallen in love with him. Had loved him almost from the first, seeing how much he'd mourned his wife and daughter. How sweet he was toward his niece, Lizzy. The way he cared about the tiny patients they operated on, took their deaths so hard. The way he'd freely admitted he had been wrong about Tristan.

The way he'd grieved for Sarah.

Even his stubborn insistence on treating *her* like a woman instead of a colleague. His protective nature was sweet.

She wanted to fight. To make him understand. But how could she fight a ghost? The horrible things she'd said to him haunted her.

When her stomach cramped, she took several deep breaths to relax. This much stress wasn't healthy. Right now she needed to take care of herself and the tiny life growing in her womb.

But she couldn't help wishing she could give her baby what every child deserved.

A loving family.

Physically, Naomi felt a little better over the next few days but decided she still needed to talk to Rick about her schedule. Especially now, in these first few months, she didn't want to do anything that might risk her pregnancy.

She and Rick needed to talk. Soon. She'd tried to get in touch with him the previous day, but he had been on trauma call and too busy to talk.

She hoped he wasn't avoiding her, but as they hadn't spoken since that disastrous confrontation in her living room, she wasn't sure.

It was her turn to be in the PICU during the day on Thursday so, armed with toast and cheese, a combination that seemed to settle her stomach the best, she headed into work.

Over the past few weeks, since their trip to Chicago, she'd fallen into the habit of avoiding Rick. Being near him was too painful after the way he'd refused to give their relationship a chance.

Now that she knew how it felt, she wished she could go back and do things differently.

She needed to find him. There was plenty of time, though. First she'd make rounds on the PICU patients.

Her pager went off halfway through rounds. She read the text message with trepidation. Sixteen-year-old female had crashed her car into a tree—multiple fractures and closed cranial trauma.

Fearing the worst, Naomi headed down to the trauma room, where treatment was already in progress.

Rick showed up a few minutes later. There wasn't time to talk, so she kept her attention centered on the patient. Jennifer's injuries were extensive. "As soon as she has a decent blood pressure I want a CT of her head."

The nurse doing the documentation nodded.

Naomi turned to the social worker. "Have you heard from the parents? Did the police get in touch with them?"

"They contacted the mother first, but are still trying to reach her dad. Parents are divorced but have joint custody."

"Let me know when her mother gets here."

"Ready to go for a CT scan," the recording nurse, Cassie, informed her.

"Good. Get her a bed in the PICU so we can go straight up afterward." Naomi glanced at Rick. "Do you have any other suggestions?"

"No." He shook his head. "You've covered all the bases."

"Dr Horton? Sally Hicks, Jennifer's mother, is here."

She drew in a deep breath. "All right. I'll need a private conference room to talk to her."

The social worker nodded, and quickly made the arrangements.

Sally Hicks was a plump woman who had obviously been crying. "How is she?" she asked, the moment Naomi walked in.

"Jennifer's condition is very serious." Naomi's heart wrenched as the woman's face crumpled. "I'm sorry, but you need to know she has several fractures in her lower legs and she's getting a CT scan of her head right now so we can find out the extent of her head injury."

Jennifer's mother broke down. The social worker put a comforting arm around her shoulders.

"Excuse me." A nurse poked her head into the conference room. "I have Jennifer's father here."

"Bring him in," Naomi instructed.

Sally lifted her head. "No. I don't want him in here."

Oh, boy. "Mrs. Hicks, if Jennifer's father has joint custody, he deserves to be here."

A man entered the conference room, his expression wild. "Jenny? Where's my daughter?"

"Mr Hicks, I'm Dr Horton." Naomi quickly introduced herself. "Jennifer is in Radiology, getting a CT scan of her head. We don't know the extent of her head injury yet, but as soon as she gets settled in the PICU, you'll both be able to go up and see her."

"I don't want Gerald to see her." Sally spoke up. "This is all his fault."

"My fault?" Gerald spun toward his ex-wife. "Why? Because she's been spending this week with me, it's my fault she hit a tree?"

"You don't keep a close eye on her, you let her do whatever she wants," Sally accused, her tears drying up with the force of her fury. The two stared at each other with thinly veiled hostility.

Naomi stepped between the parents, hiding her own annoyance. "Stop it, both of you. Jennifer is very sick. She's going to need both of her parents to be strong."

They backed off, but the tension in the room didn't lessen much.

After much debate the parents agreed on alternate visiting. Naomi was glad, but still hoped the two would come together for Jennifer's sake.

Rick walked into the conference room. He caught her gaze, silently asking if she needed help. Obviously, he'd heard the commotion between the parents.

Giving her head a slight shake, she turned back towards the warring parents. "If either of you interferes with Jennifer's care we'll have you escorted out and you'll lose your visiting privileges."

The parents fell silent, realizing it wasn't an idle threat.

She left the conference room to go and check on

Jennifer's CT scan results. She couldn't bear to look at Rick.

She felt sick. Was this the sort of relationship they had in store for them? Fighting over the well-being of their child?

She wouldn't let him throw away what they had.

Rick didn't have time to talk to Naomi for the rest of the day. Jennifer's condition took a turn for the worse and he ended up consulting Neurosurgery to put an intracranial pressure monitoring device in.

So far the parents were behaving themselves, but he wasn't totally certain the tentative truce between them would last.

As he was on call, he took over Jennifer's care. After Naomi filled him in on what they'd done so far, they made rounds rather quickly on the other patients in the unit so he could return to Jennifer's room.

Watching the Hicks parents fighting had made him realize he and Naomi needed to mend the rift between them. Anger was useless.

As far as Naomi getting pregnant went, she was right. Placing blame on a defective condom wasn't going to change anything.

They had a baby to plan for. Not just the birth, but afterward. Somehow, some way, they needed to make this work.

He frowned. He refused to make the same mistakes all over again.

Naomi looked exhausted by the end of the day, so he gladly let her go home. There was no way she'd be able to keep up the fast trauma pace while being pregnant.

Would she be upset if he suggested she cut down to a part-time status? Probably, but hopefully in the long run she'd realize he was only doing this because he cared about her.

He didn't get much sleep that night, between thinking of Naomi and their baby and the seemingly nonstop trauma calls. Most of the calls weren't serious, but they were spaced just enough a part to interrupt his ability to get a decent block of sleep.

Jennifer's condition had stabilized by morning. He kept her sedated and paralyzed to help control the swelling in her brain. Leaving the pretty young girl wasn't easy. He already found himself emotionally involved with her, maybe because her parents were being so ridiculous. When his vision kept blurring, though, he realized he wasn't helping anyone by staying.

He reluctantly left Jennifer in Debra's capable care and headed home.

After five hours of sleep, he dragged himself out of bed, still somewhat groggy but feeling far more functional. He would have liked to have slept longer, but knew that he also needed to get back on a regular schedule. There was nothing worse than getting your days and nights totally mixed up.

Babies tended to do that to you. He couldn't help but smile when he remembered those first few weeks after they'd brought Sarah home. Babies never cared whether it was day or night, and sleep-deprived parents made it their mission to get their infant on a regular sleep schedule.

His smile faded.

Was Naomi right? He'd been emotionally distant since losing Gabrielle and Sarah, but had he been the same way during his marriage?

Gabrielle had claimed he was, but he'd thought her accusation had been part of her not wanting to be alone.

Maybe he'd been wrong. About a lot of things.

He picked up his cell phone and called Naomi's number. No answer. Instead, the call went directly to voicemail.

She didn't have her cell phone on.

Was she working?

He called the PICU and asked for the attending on service. The charge nurse told him Debra Maloney was in the middle of putting in a chest tube. Unwilling to interrupt her, he hung up.

Maybe Naomi was at home, sleeping. Or sick again. He knew for a fact she'd been sick again during the day she'd admitted Jennifer from the trauma room. At one point she'd bolted from the room, only to return about fifteen minutes later, munching on a piece of dry toast.

Concerned, he once again headed to Naomi's house. This time he wouldn't get angry. This time they'd have a normal, constructive conversation.

About the present. And the future. About what was best for their unborn child.

And for the two of them.

When he pulled into Naomi's driveway, her garage door was closed, as if she wasn't home. With a frown he got out and marched up to the front door, knocking and ringing the doorbell.

He hated to wake her up if she was sleeping, but it was only six o'clock in the evening.

When there was no response, he returned to his car and called the PICU again. This time he waited for Debra to respond.

"Debra? Rick. Hey, I'm looking for Naomi. Have you seen her? Wasn't she supposed to be on call tonight?"

"Dirk is actually coming in to cover for her," Debra admitted. "She fainted, Rick. Right in the middle of the operating room. We sent her over to the E.D. at Trinity Medical Center."

"She fainted?" His stomach clenched, remembering what she'd told him about her miscarriage. The heavy bleeding, the need for surgery and blood transfusions.

"She recovered quickly enough, don't worry." Debra must have sensed his concern.

"Is she still at the hospital?" he demanded.

"As far as I know, she is. Last we heard they were planning to admit her overnight for observation."

Dear heaven. Was she all right? The baby? He didn't waste a second.

He snapped his phone shut and started the car, heading straight for Trinity Medical Center.

CHAPTER FOURTEEN

NAOMI tipped her head back against the pillow and closed her eyes.

She was so exhausted. At least now she knew why. All her electrolytes were completely out of whack from her constant nausea. According to the doctor, she had hyperemesis after all. She hadn't imagined the symptoms.

She should have listened to what her body had been telling her.

"Are you doing all right?" the nurse, Melanie, asked for what seemed like the third time.

She opened her eyes and forced a smile. "Fine. Just tired."

Melanie rolled her eyes and nodded. "Yes, the first trimester is awful, isn't it?"

The way Melanie spoke, as if she'd been there recently, made Naomi ask, "Are you pregnant, too?"

"Yes. I'm about twenty weeks along." Melanie flashed a pair of adorable dimples. "I feel so much better now, than I did earlier. Hang in there. I'm sure you'll feel better soon, too."

Melanie hardly looked at all pregnant, but then again it was difficult to tell in the baggy scrubs.

She looked down at her own stomach, hoping and praying the baby was fine. When she'd suddenly fainted at work, she'd realized something serious had been wrong. She'd quickly called her doctor and gone straight to the emergency department. At first she'd been scared, but when the doctor had come in he'd told her there was no reason to think she'd lost the baby. Still, she wouldn't be satisfied until they told her for certain.

She hadn't argued over being admitted overnight as an inpatient.

Rick. Heavens, she'd totally forgotten to call Rick. She reached for her cell phone and saw several missed messages.

From him.

He'd been trying to get in touch with her. Ridiculous tears threatened again and she blinked them away. What was wrong with her? She didn't like feeling so weepy. Stupid hormones.

"Naomi?" Rick burst in through the door, seemingly out of breath, as if he'd run the whole way, his gaze zeroing in on her like a dog scenting its prey. He crossed over to her, took her hand in his, and raked his gaze over her. "What happened? You fainted? Are you really all right?"

"I'm fine." Strange he didn't immediately ask about the baby. She clutched his hand, grateful for his strength and support. "And so is the baby, at least from what we know. It's too early to hear the heartbeat but they're talking about doing an ultrasound to confirm everything is still good." She hoped they'd do the ultra-sound tonight, but it might have to wait until morning.

"What about you?" He seemed to have a one-track mind. She couldn't squelch the tiny surge of hope. Maybe he did care about her, at least a little. "Any bleeding?"

"No bleeding." Had he assumed she'd already had a miscarriage?

"Thank heavens." His heartfelt relief was palpable. Then he frowned. "So why did you faint?"

"My electrolytes are messed up." She grimaced and waved a hand toward the IV bag hanging on the pump beside her. "Hyperemesis. I'm on my second liter of IV fluid, including extra potassium." She didn't add that her potassium levels had been dangerously low to the point she'd had several premature ventricular beats which had contributed to her fainting spell.

"So you're okay." He didn't release her hand but sank into the chair next to her bed. "You're really all right."

His concern was heart-warming. "I'm fine. Really."

"God, Naomi, I was so scared." He stared down at the floor for a moment. "I thought you were hemor-rhaging when Debra told me you fainted in the middle of the operating room." He raked his free hand over his face. "I went a little crazy. I was so worried about you."

"I'm fine." The fainting spell had been mortifying. Good thing the anesthesiologist on duty had managed to call for back-up. Debra had assured her that the patient on the O.R. table was fine with no ill effects from his surgeon having collapse on the floor.

"I'm sorry you were worried. I guess I should have gone to see the doctor right away, with how sick I've been."

He nodded and then lifted his gaze to meet hers. "Why didn't you call me?"

Good question. "I don't know why it took me so long to think of it." She held up her cell phone. "I was about to call when you came in."

He stared at her. "As the baby's father, I'd have thought you'd call me right away."

"I know." Helplessly she lifted a shoulder. "I guess subconsciously I was afraid. The last time we spoke you were pretty angry."

"That's no excuse." He scowled. "I'd never hurt you."

Closing her eyes, she sighed. She wished things were different. That they were a loving couple instead of being constantly at odds. She couldn't stand knowing that the only reason he was here was because of the baby. How had something as beautiful as their lovemaking gone so wrong? "I don't know if I can do this," she whispered, looking over at him. "I don't want things to be awful between us."

He didn't answer.

She had to try to make him understand. "Rick, I can't change the past. I did consider having a baby on my own. When Andrew left me…" She paused, swallowed hard. "He hurt me. Said he'd considered leaving me because of my schedule, but made the decision for certain when he found out about my difficulties with conceiving a baby."

"If he loved you, that wouldn't have mattered."

Her smile was sad. "Yes, I know. And that was the real problem. He didn't love me. I think in some ways he was relieved when I lost the baby. It was a good excuse for him to move on. To a life with someone more…compatible."

Rick's hand tightened around hers. "I'm sorry. He should have been a better husband to you."

Yes, she had deserved better, it was easy to see that now. "I changed my mind. Because, as much as I wanted a baby, I discovered I really wanted something more." She forced herself to look up. "I wanted to create a new life out of a loving relationship, not artificial methods. But I also wanted the whole package, a husband and a family." She met his gaze. "I know it's all messed up and confused now, but a tiny part of me hoped that I'd found the beginning of a beautiful relationship in Chicago."

He let out his breath on a heavy sigh. "And then I told you I wasn't ready."

"Yes." It still hurt to remember that moment when he'd pulled away emotionally and let her go. That weekend in Chicago had held some of the most wonderful moments in her life. And also the most painful. Worse than when Andrew had left her, because deep down she'd known things hadn't been good between her and Andrew. But with Rick, everything had just felt…different.

"I understand, I really do," she said finally. "Losing your wife and daughter was devastating. But you can't ask me to pretend things are great between us when they aren't."

"What would you say if I asked for another chance?" A hint of uncertainty shadowed his gaze.

She wished it were that easy. But he couldn't possibly have gotten over his feelings toward his wife and daughter so quickly. "I'd say you were willing to do anything for the sake of our baby. And I deserve better. I deserve to be loved for who I am, not just because of our child."

Rick watched Naomi long after she fell asleep, her beautiful features relaxed and peaceful.

If only his gut would stop churning with anxiety.

She didn't believe him. He'd asked for a second chance and she'd dismissed his attempt to reconcile, assuming it was only because of the baby.

He shifted in the recliner, never taking his gaze from Naomi. Thinking of losing her had sent him into a panic. He didn't even remember the drive from her house to Trinity. He'd broken every rule of their road safety campaign. He'd called the hospital to find out which room she was in and had been relieved when he'd finally seen her and she'd seemed to be fine.

Of course he cared about the baby. But Naomi was more important. They could always try again to have a child.

He loved her.

Love. He caught his breath at the revelation. Why had it taken so long to sink in? He was in love. With Naomi.

The knowledge didn't scare him. Didn't make him want to bolt from the hospital room.

Just the opposite. Knowing he loved Naomi made him want to fight. To win the woman he loved.

Acknowledging the truth felt good. He grinned like an idiot in the darkness. He should have realized long before now. It shouldn't have taken hearing Debra tell him about Naomi fainting for him to come to grips with his emotions.

Her pregnancy had knocked him backward, no doubt about it. He had just been coming to terms with his feelings for her when she'd thrown the baby into the mix.

A wife and a child. A second chance. For a moment his heart tightened painfully in his chest. Could he do it again? Walk down the path of having a family?

What if something awful happened? To Naomi? Or to the baby?

What if he screwed up again?

He turned his head to look at her. Whether Naomi walked away from him now or he lost her at some other time, the intense grief would be the same.

There was no point in going through life thinking the worst. If he did that, then he'd never bother to operate on a severely injured child. Miracles happened all the time; badly injured kids recovered from devastating situations.

Naomi had called this pregnancy a miracle. He believed her when she claimed the doctor had told her she might not conceive again. Yet somehow, during that weekend in Chicago, one of the happiest times in his life, she had. And now she was going to have their baby. His baby.

Somehow he had to make her understand how much he loved her.

And convince her to give him a second chance.

Naomi was surprised to discover Rick was still there in the morning, sleeping in the recliner beside her. She snuck out of bed to go to the bathroom, and barely made it back before a woman pushing a large, bulky machine entered the room.

"Good morning. My name is Claire-Ann and I'm one of the ultrasound techs working in Radiology." She flashed a bright smile. "I'm here to perform your ultrasound procedure."

She sucked in a quick breath and glanced with trepidation at Rick, who had just woken up. "Already? Where's Dr Goldman? Shouldn't he be here, too?"

"He ordered the procedure, but it didn't say anything about having him nearby." Claire-Ann gave a little frown as she glanced down at the slip of paper in her hand. "Do you want me to call him first?"

"Would you, please?" She couldn't hide her fear. What if this technologist told her everything was all right when it really wasn't? Or vice versa? She knew she was being ridiculous, but she'd feel much better if Dr Goldman was there to read the results correctly. She glanced over at Rick who immediately picked up on her concern.

"Hey, what's wrong?" Rick sat up and reached for her hand again. "You're really worried about this procedure, aren't you?"

"A little."

"I'm here for you, don't worry."

"I know." She didn't want to tell him the extent of her anxiety. Since she'd been admitted she hadn't felt that awful nausea any more. What if the missing nausea was a sign that she'd lost the baby? Although she hadn't noticed any bleeding, she still couldn't be sure. Sometimes the bleeding didn't start for a few days.

"I'm sure the baby is fine." He gently squeezed her hand. "And if something did happen, we'll try again."

Try again? She stared at him. Was he serious?

He must have read her confusion. "Hey, I know you thought this baby was a miracle, but if you managed to get pregnant once, I'm sure with a little effort we can make it happen again."

He was talking as if they had a future. As if they were a couple.

Just then Claire-Ann came back in. "Dr Goldman is on his way, he'll be here in a few minutes." Claire-Ann bustled about, hooking the machine up and getting things ready.

Naomi clung to Rick's hand when Claire-Ann lifted her hospital gown to reveal Naomi's abdomen.

"The gel is cold," she warned as she squirted a blob onto her belly.

She didn't mind the cold, but stared at the ultrasound screen, trying to read it for herself as Claire-Ann moved the wand over her stomach.

"Good morning." Dr Goldman entered the room. "Have you found the fetus yet?"

"We just got started," Claire-Ann said as she continued moving the wand.

They couldn't see the baby. Naomi froze, feeling sick. Dear heaven, they couldn't find a baby.

"There it is," Dr Goldman said, putting his hand over Claire-Ann's to stop the movement. "There, can you see it?"

"Yes!" Naomi squinted at the screen. "Can you tell me the baby's gender?"

"No. Don't tell us," Rick said quickly.

She looked at him in surprise. "Why not?"

He lifted a shoulder. "Because it doesn't matter as long as it's healthy. I'm more concerned about your health, especially now."

Dr Goldman smiled. "Good attitude. But, actually, it's too early to tell the baby's gender. Can't see that until about sixteen weeks." He picked up her chart. "Your electrolytes are almost back to normal, and the medication we gave you for the nausea seems to be working. And from what I can see here…" he gestured to the ultrasound screen "…your baby is healthy too."

"Really?" Hope filled her heart. "I'm glad."

"If you really want to know the gender, we can schedule another ultrasound a little further on."

Maybe she would. She watched the blip on the screen as they measured the baby and verified her due date. The procedure was over before she knew it.

"I'll discharge you home today on one condition," Dr Goldman told her.

"What?" Rick asked, as if she wasn't able to speak for herself. She glanced at him in exasperation.

"That she takes the anti-nausea medication if she gets sick more than once per day."

"I don't want to take medicine and risk the baby," she said, ignoring Rick.

"This medication is fine. There are no side effects that will harm the baby. And you don't need to take it unless things get bad."

"She'll take it," Rick said. "Anything else?"

"Come back to see me in two weeks." Dr Goldman glanced from her to Rick. "Any questions, call me."

"We will."

She waited until Dr Goldman had left, before rounding on him. "We? Just because you stayed the night with me, it doesn't mean you get to call all the shots around here," she snapped.

"I love you."

What? She blinked. Was he just saying that to get her to shut up?

"I know I've acted like a jerk, especially when you first told me about the baby, but it's true. I love you, Naomi. With or without the baby, I love you. I think I fell in love with you the moment you disobeyed my orders not to move Tristan into Emily's room."

Stunned, she didn't know what to say.

"You need to have a little faith. In me. In my love for you." He stared at her.

"I know you care about the baby," she admitted slowly. "But I don't want you to stay with me just because I'm pregnant." Marriage was difficult enough. She'd already gone through one divorce, she didn't plan on going through another. "I deserve more."

"More than my love for you? I want to marry you. To have a family with you." His tone was serious. "I made a lot of mistakes with Gabrielle. I've been afraid of making them all over again. Will you, please, give me another chance?"

She hesitated, hope warring with doubt. From the moment he'd come into her hospital room he'd been more worried about her than about the baby. And then he'd made it sound as if they had a future, regardless of whether the baby survived or not. Yet at the same time she didn't want to compete with ghosts from his past. "What about your feelings for Gabrielle and Sarah?"

"I'll always miss them, but you were right in that they taught me a very important lesson. I have been emotionally distant and that's wrong. Because one thing Gabrielle and Sarah taught me was how to love." He stood and came to sit beside her on the bed. "And I love you, Naomi. Very much."

"I love you, too." Her infernal hormones kicked in and her eyes misted with tears. "But you'd better pinch me so I know I'm not dreaming."

"No pinching." He smiled. "I'm going to step down as Chief of Trauma. I refuse to allow my career to be more important than my family. We'll work out our schedules so that our marriage and our children come first."

She caught her breath. "You'd do that for me?"

"For us." He pulled her close and kissed her. Not just a quick peck on the cheek but a full kiss, one that promised more. "I'll do anything for us."

She understood. Because, when you loved someone, compromise wasn't too much to ask.

"I love you, Rick." She kissed him again, wishing they were home, in bed. Soon. Once they decided where they were going to live. She sighed, full of contentment. "I'd still like to know the sex of our child."

He shook his head, holding her close. "We'll see. I think I'd rather be surprised."

EPILOGUE

"Come on, sweetheart, push. You're almost there," Rick encouraged.

Naomi resisted the urge to snap at him. Easy for him to tell her to push. Beads of sweat poured down her face, dampening her hospital gown. The agonizing pain was more than she'd bargained for, yet it was too late to turn back now.

She gritted her teeth as the next contraction crested. Breathing through the pain, she pushed.

"That's it. The head is out. One more push and the rest of the baby will be born," Dr Goldman said in a calm tone.

She groaned under her breath, but pushed again. Just when she didn't think she could take a second more, the pressure eased. She sat back, breathing heavily.

"It's a boy. Naomi and Rick, you have a beautiful baby boy."

"A son." Rick laughed, but his eyes were suspiciously bright as he bent down to kiss her. "Sweetheart, we have a son."

"Joseph Richard Weber," she whispered in awe. They'd already chosen baby names for both a girl and a boy. Joseph was Rick's middle name and she thought it was fitting to name their son after his father.

They'd gotten married several months ago in a small quiet ceremony at her church. Jess had stood up as her matron of honor and Lizzy had been thrilled to be bridesmaid. Dirk had been Rick's best man and the rest of the trauma surgeons, except for Chuck who had held down the fort at the hospital, had been there as well.

Frank had been named the interim medical director after Rick had stepped down. Administration had tried to convince Rick to stay on, offering to bend the rules so they could be married, but he'd refused.

In a way she was glad. They both enjoyed their careers, but they had also agreed it was time to focus on love and family.

"I love you, Naomi," Rick murmured, resting his forehead against hers.

"I love you, too." When Dr Goldman put Joseph into her arms, she gazed down at his tiny face, awed all over again at the miracle of life.

She was the luckiest woman in the world to have a loving husband and a new son.

The family she'd always wanted.

Medical Romance™

COMING NEXT MONTH
TO MEDICAL ROMANCE SUBSCRIBERS

Visit www.eHarlequin.com for more details.

A PROPOSAL WORTH WAITING FOR by Lilian Darcy
Crocodile Creek 24-Hour Rescue
Surgeon Nick Devlin knows he's neglected his son, but going with him to Crocodile Creek Kids' Camp will change that. Nick is the last person Miranda expects to see there—their one passionate night at medical school left her with heartache, and she's determined to keep her distance….

THE SPANISH DOCTOR'S LOVE-CHILD by Kate Hardy
Mediterranean Doctors
Career-driven doctor Leandro Herrera never becomes emotionally involved with women. But then he discovers his new nurse is Becky Marston—the woman he spent one passionate night with…. And Becky announces she's pregnant! Suddenly the hot-blooded Spanish doctor wants the mother of his child as his wife!

A DOCTOR, A NURSE: A LITTLE MIRACLE by Carol Marinelli
Nurse Molly Jones has discovered that pediatrician Luke Williams is back—with four-year-old twins! Single dad Luke is charming—but Molly's heart was broken when Luke left, and when she discovered that, for her, motherhood was never meant to be.

TOP-NOTCH SURGEON, PREGNANT NURSE by Amy Andrews
Nursing manager Beth Rogers forgot her past for one amazing night, not expecting to see her English lover again. He turns out to be hotshot surgeon Gabe Fallon—and they'll be working together to save two tiny girls! Then Beth discovers she's carrying his baby.

HMEDCNM0808

Thoroughbred Legacy

The purse is set and the stakes are high...

Romance, scandal and glamour set in the exhilarating world of horse racing!

Follow the 12-book continuity, in September with:

Millions to Spare
by BARBARA DUNLOP
Book #5

Courting Disaster
by KATHLEEN O'REILLY
Book #6

Who's Cheatin' Who?
by MAGGIE PRICE
Book #7

A Lady's Luck
by KEN CASPER
Book #8